Treasure at First Base

BOOKS BY ELEANOR CLYMER

A YARD FOR JOHN

HERE COMES PETE

THE GROCERY MOUSE

LITTLE BEAR ISLAND

THE TROLLEY CAR FAMILY

THE LATCH-KEY CLUB

THE COUNTRY KITTENS

TREASURE AT FIRST BASE

TREASURE
AT FIRST BASE

BY ELEANOR CLYMER

ILLUSTRATED BY JEAN MACDONALD PORTER

DODD, MEAD & COMPANY · NEW YORK · 1957

Manufactured by
The Cornwall Press, Inc., Cornwall, N. Y.
Designed by Stefan Salter

Published May, 1950
Second printing August, 1950
Third printing November, 1950
Fourth printing, September, 1951
Fifth printing, October, 1954
Sixth printing, July, 1957

Contents

Illustrations

To Adam

Without Whose Expert Advice on Baseball

This Book Could Not Have Been Written

1. Baseball Weather

JOHNNY BURTON lay in bed, waiting for his mother to call up the stairs to tell him it was time to get up.

Lying there, he looked around his room as he had done every morning for two months—ever since the Burtons had moved to the country. It was a nice room, larger than his old room in the city. The walls were covered with pennants and pictures of baseball players. A bat stood in a corner and a glove hung on a nail. Johnny's eyes rested fondly on these things. He yawned. He would have to get up in a few minutes and do his chores, but he liked to lie in bed for a little while first.

Through the window he could look out across the roof of the barn and the chicken house, over fields and gently rising hills. The branches of an apple tree waved outside the window. They had been bare when the Burtons came, but now it was April and they were covered with pink-and-white blossoms. A breeze came in and blew over Johnny. It smelled good.

Downstairs Johnny could hear his mother in the kitchen, walking back and forth, making noises with dishes. He could smell coffee and bacon.

He heard a car horn toot, and the door of the store banging and then his father's steps on the brick walk. That meant somebody was stopping for gasoline. Pretty soon he heard his father coming in again, talking to his mother. Their voices sounded happy. They liked it out here. His father was always saying how much nicer it was than being in a crowded city and how lucky they were to have found a place like this.

The house was an old wooden farmhouse, with the front room made into a store. Out back were the barn and the chicken house, and in front, at the edge of the road, were two gasoline pumps.

It was just right for the Burton family. They could live in the house and sell groceries and eggs in the store. Johnny's father could do some car-re-pair work, and Johnny and his mother could raise vegetables in the garden.

Johnny hadn't been sure at first that he would like living in the country. He was a great baseball fan. In the city he and his friends played in the street every day after school. They saved up their money and went to the ball games every week. Johnny didn't know whether he would get as much baseball in the country as he did in the city.

His mother and father had pointed out that, while he might not see so many ball games, he would probably have just as many chances to play, if not more. The farm was only two miles away from the town of Willow Creek where Johnny would go to school. Boys everywhere played baseball, so naturally the Willow Creek boys would play baseball, too. And probably there would be lots more space to play than in the city. So Johnny was waiting for a chance to play.

So far he hadn't had any. The weather had been terrible ever since they had come. It had rained or snowed, or it had been too cold to go out without an overcoat on. And then there had been mud. You couldn't play ball with a ton of galoshes on your feet.

The other boys in Johnny's class hadn't seemed to

care too much. They were nice fellows. Johnny got along with them fine. But they were always busy playing Indians, and when Johnny spoke about baseball they didn't pay much attention.

Johnny had decided that it was because it wasn't the baseball season yet. Though it *was* a little funny. The boys in the city talked a lot about baseball, even when they couldn't play. But not these Willow Creek boys. As soon as school was out they started playing Indians. He'd never seen kids so fond of playing Indians.

He'd mentioned it to his mother once, and she had said, "Well, you know this was once Indian country. Probably those boys' ancestors really did fight Indians right around here."

"Well, even so," Johnny had said, "the boys don't have to keep on doing it. They could play something else."

Johnny had played Indians when he was little, but he wasn't much interested in the game now.

Again that breeze came in through the open window, fluttering the curtains. It smelled of apple blossoms and ploughed ground. It smelled quite different from any city breeze. What was it?

Johnny sat up and looked out of the window to

see what it was that made that breeze smell so good.

And suddenly he knew! It was spring!

It was a perfectly wonderful day!

This was no kind of morning to be lying in bed, waiting for Mother to call him. It was baseball weather!

Johnny jumped out of bed and put his clothes on fast. He ran to the bathroom and washed the front of his face. He didn't bother about the sides. He snatched up his books and his ball and glove and ran downstairs. The kitchen clock said seven.

His father looked up as he came in.

"Good morning, son," he said. "Nice to see you so early."

His mother smiled. "I usually have to call you

two or three times," she said.

"My gosh! Not on a day like this!" Johnny exclaimed. "It's baseball weather! Pop, if I hurry up with the chores, will you have a catch with me after breakfast?"

"Why, of course," his father said. "Got all your homework done?"

Johnny said, "Mm." It was true that he could have studied his history lesson *harder,* but he didn't want to go into that now.

His mother began to break eggs into a bowl.

Johnny ate his breakfast in a hurry and ran out to feed the chickens. He scattered the corn on the ground, and when they all rushed to pick it up he went into the chicken house to get the eggs. There were fourteen eggs. He put them into the empty feed pail and went back to the house. He brought in an armful of stove wood and then ran to the store, where his father was arranging cans of tomatoes on a shelf.

"Come on, Pop," he said. "It's a quarter to eight. We have half an hour before the school bus comes."

Mr. Burton called to his wife, "Mary! Will you mind the store for a few minutes? We boys are going out for practice."

Johnny went into the chicken house to get the eggs

They went down the porch steps, past the red gasoline pumps and across the road.

There, opposite the farmhouse, was a little house. It was very small. It looked more like a playhouse than anything that grown-ups would think of using. Johnny's father used it as a storage room for extra groceries.

It was built of stone—the same kind of rough limestone that lay about in the fields.

There were some odd things about it. It had a front door that opened on the road—just an ordinary pine door. That was all right. But it had a back door that was made of heavy oak planks. That door was locked, and nobody ever opened it. There were no windows on the front, looking out on the road, where you might expect windows to be. But there were two little windows, one on either side of the back door.

When the Burtons had come to Willow Creek, almost the first thing Johnny had done was to explore the little house and ask what it was.

His father didn't know. He thought the neighbors might know. But the neighbors only said, "Oh, that! That's the old store. Always was the store before they started using the front of the house for that. Handy, too, right on the road."

But who had built it and why, the neighbors didn't know.

Johnny's father thought it might originally have been the farmhouse. They didn't have time to build big houses in the old pioneer days, and this little house was no bigger than a log cabin.

"But then," said Johnny, "how did they have time to build a stone house? That would take a lot of time."

His father agreed. In the old days, when they were first settling this country, everybody built log cabins. A stone house would have taken much too long when they had Indians to fight, and a clearing to make and corn to plant. So the stone house must have been built later. But, then, why was it so small? All the later houses were good and big.

It was a puzzle the Burtons could not solve.

There was another curious thing. A brook flowed along right behind the little stone house. It flowed in a deep ditch so that if you *had* managed to get the back door open, you would have found yourself at the top of a high bank with the brook at the bottom. In order to get over to the field on the other side, you would have had to take a good long jump or fall into the water.

Why, Johnny wondered, should anybody build a house with a back door right over a brook?

The brook was Willow Creek. It gurgled along beside the road and across the fields, and then on through the center of the town. The town was named for the brook, and the brook was named for the willows that grew along its banks. There was one huge willow on the other side of the stream, just behind the little house. Its branches arched over the water and drooped on the roof.

At one side of the little house was a wooden foot-bridge, by which one could get across the brook and into the field behind the house.

Now Johnny and his father crossed the bridge and walked out into the middle of the field.

"All right," said Mr. Burton, "get over there and let's see if you still remember how to throw."

"If *I* still remember!" said Johnny. "All right, Pop, get this one."

He placed his knuckles on the ball and let fly. Mr. Burton reached for it, but, just as it seemed to be falling into his hands, it took a turn and fell on the ground.

Mr. Burton laughed. "I'd forgotten that curve

ball of yours," he said. "Never mind the tricks now. Let's have some good fast ones."

He shot one to his son and Johnny shot it right back again. They played until they were both warm and out of breath.

"We'd better take a rest now," said Mr. Burton.

But just then a horn tooted in the road.

"It's the bus!" Johnny yelled. "Good-bye, Pop! I might be late coming home. Maybe I'll stay and play ball!"

He ran across the bridge, seized his books, lunch and baseball glove, and jumped on board the bus.

2.

No Ball Game Today

JOHNNY dropped into a seat and wiped his sweating face. Then the bus started, and he looked around and said hello to the people he knew. He didn't know any of them very well. There were several first graders, and some girls and a few big boys in the eighth grade, who came from Spring Hill, about five miles away. Most of the boys in Johnny's class lived right in town and just walked to school.

The bus rolled along the smooth road. Johnny looked out of the window. Cows were grazing in the fields. There were sheep, too; some of them with baby lambs that jumped around, stiff-legged, as if they were glad to be out on such a nice day.

The fruit trees were all in bloom.

Johnny felt good. Spring was certainly here.

Now they were coming into town. They passed some red brick buildings in the midst of wide lawns. Young men in leather jackets or sweaters were walking around there. It was Hollister College. Some of the young men had tennis rackets under their arms. And there were some with baseball bats! Johnny turned in his seat to stare after them as the bus rolled past.

Now they were turning into School Street. The bus stopped in front of the big white building, and everybody jumped out. Johnny ran to the corner of the yard where his friends always waited. There were five of them, sitting on the ground, playing mumblety-peg.

There was Buster Evans, a thin boy with glasses. He didn't look much like a buster, but that was what they called him. There were the Williams twins, Howard and Charles. There was Joe Palo, and there was Max Schlussel, who had lived in Poland until his aunt and uncle brought him to Willow Creek. He couldn't speak English very well yet but he was trying awfully hard to learn.

"Hi!" said Johnny, rushing up to them.

"Hello," said Buster. "Want to play?"

Johnny said, "We-ell, I was thinking, how about playing ball a little, till the bell rings?"

Max jumped up and said, "All right. I will play." He was always ready to oblige.

But the others didn't move.

"We haven't got room here," said Joe.

Johnny looked around the yard. It *was* getting pretty crowded.

"Can't we go out in the street?" he asked.

The boys shook their heads. "Not allowed."

"Oh, well, how about after school? I brought my glove. What do you say we go out for a game?"

Buster nodded. "OK," he said. "Or we could play Indians."

Howard and Charles brightened up. "We've got a new tent," said Howard. "Pa gave us a big piece of canvas."

Johnny stared at them. "Hey, don't you ever talk about anything but Indians?" he asked.

"Sure," said Buster, surprised. "What do you mean?"

"I mean baseball," said Johnny. "Where I come from they play baseball."

"Oh, sure we play ball," said Joe. "My brother Tony is gonna teach me. He plays with his gang."

"Well, couldn't we go out this afternoon and play with them?" Johnny asked.

The boys shook their heads.

"No," said Joe. "We can't play with the big boys. They wouldn't let us."

"Why not?"

"Oh, there isn't enough room," said Joe.

"Where do they play?" Johnny asked.

"Over on Oak Street, in the empty lot."

"Well, let's go over and play this afternoon."

"No, we can't."

"But why not?" Johnny insisted.

"They wouldn't let us," said Joe.

"But they don't own the lot, do they?" Johnny demanded.

"No, but they always play there," Buster explained. "So they wouldn't want us to come butting in."

His explanation didn't make much sense to Johnny. "Well, where do you guys play?" he asked.

"Well, we mostly play catch in somebody's yard," said Buster.

"And we play Indians," said Howard.

Johnny shook his head. He couldn't understand it at all. Just then the bell rang and they all went inside.

Johnny kept stealing glances toward the window. The sky was still blue and the breeze still smelled wonderful. But he had to sit here and listen to the teacher asking dull questions and the children giving dull answers. Buster was saying something about Little Turtle. Why were they talking about turtles, anyhow? This wasn't nature class. He waited to hear what Buster would say.

"In 1891," said Buster, "Little Turtle beat General St. Clair."

Johnny suddenly realized that Little Turtle

wasn't a turtle. He was an Indian.

"That's right," said the teacher. "And just think! All this fighting was going on right in this state; in fact, not very far from here. Only the country didn't look the way it does now. It was all deep woods, except where the settlers had made a few clearings. And what kind of houses did they live in?"

"Log cabins," Howard called out. "And the Indians were all around in the woods."

My goodness, Johnny thought. No wonder these kids played Indians all the time. They heard so much about them at school!

Suddenly his thoughts were interrupted. The teacher was calling his name.

"John!"

"Yes, ma'am!" said Johnny, getting up.

"You seem to be watching something outside the window," said the teacher. "You don't seem to be with us."

"Oh, yes, I am," said Johnny. A couple of girls giggled.

"Well, then, suppose you tell us about General Anthony Wayne. What did he do about the Indians?"

"General Wayne?" said Johnny, trying to remember. "Why–uh–he–uh–" He couldn't seem to place General Anthony Wayne. The name wasn't even familiar to him. This must be the part he had not studied so well. He felt his face getting red. He shook his head unhappily.

"You may sit down," said the teacher. "And tonight perhaps you had better study a little harder."

Johnny sat down. Half the class were waving their hands in the air. Buster looked as if he would shake his arm right off. So did Joe.

"Well, Joe?" said the teacher.

"He beat the Indians at Fallen Timbers, Indiana," said Joe. "That's a place where a hurricane blew a lot of trees down. Then they made a treaty at Fort Greenville. That's the same as what Greenville is now. Then all the settlers could go ahead and settle and the Indians didn't bother them any more."

"Very good," said the teacher. "But why did the Indians make so much trouble for the white men? Wasn't there enough room for everybody?"

Again the air was filled with waving hands.

"Max, you tell us," said the teacher.

Max said slowly, choosing his words carefully,

"You see, the white men spoiled for the Indians the hunting grounds. They chopped down the trees and chased away from there the animals, the deers and the bears and the wild geeses."

Max's English was a little mixed up, but nobody laughed.

The teacher nodded and said, "That's right, Max. But the white men had to live, too, didn't they? It was a hard struggle. It's hard to say who was right." The class nodded seriously.

History was over at last. Johnny felt he had had enough of Indians to last him a month. Finally three o'clock came.

Johnny packed up his books, picked up his glove and went out with the others. At last he was going to have some fun.

Some of the big boys were walking off together. They had bats and balls.

"Come on," said Johnny to his friends. "Let's go with them. Maybe they'll let us play."

But Buster shook his head. "They wouldn't."

Joe said, "I gotta wait till my brother says I can come."

Johnny was disgusted. "Look," he said; "if you're scared to go over to Oak Street and there's no other place, why don't you all come out to my house? There's lots of room. A whole field."

But that didn't suit them either. "It's too far," said Howard. "We'd have to walk four miles."

"You come with us and play Indians," said Charles.

"No," said Johnny. "I don't want to."

He waited until they walked away. Then he turned and followed the big boys to Oak Street. He'd show them. He was going to play ball.

The bus was just starting. The driver tooted his horn at him, but Johnny waved and shock his head to show he wasn't coming.

He trotted along School Street and turned the corner. Ahead of him was the empty lot. It wasn't a very big lot. In one corner of it was a large sign that said, "This property for sale. See W. H. Townsend, Main Street." The boys used the sign for a backstop. They had a piece of chicken wire nailed across the bottom to keep balls from rolling underneath.

The big boys were starting to choose teams. Johnny recognized the captains. One was Tony, Joe's big brother, and the other was Michael Brown, one of the boys who rode in on the bus with him.

The big boys were starting to choose teams

Johnny ran over to them and called out, "Can I play?"

The boys stopped choosing and looked at him. Then Tony said in a chilly voice, "Why don't you play with the kids your size?"

Johnny felt as if somebody had given him a push. He took a step backward.

"They—they don't want to play," he stammered. "They're going to play Indians."

"Well, then *you* play Indians, too," said Tony. "Those kids can't play ball."

"But *I* can," said Johnny.

"Look," said Michael. "If we let you play, we'd have to let the others, too."

"But—" Johnny began.

"No," said Michael. "You go on. Now don't argue with me."

Johnny turned and walked away. He didn't want them to see how badly he felt. He turned the corner into School Street and started for home.

3. Andrew Jackson Sedgwick

JOHNNY tramped the two miles out from town. His books were heavy and the glove, buckled to his belt, slapped against his leg at each step. He was tired and he was hot, but most of all he was unhappy.

What a day! He had started out full of hopes in the morning, and here it was afternoon and the whole day had been wasted. Not only had there been no ballplaying, but he had no idea how he was going to play ball in the future. Why had his family had to move out here? Why couldn't they have stayed in the city, where a fellow could have some fun?

At last he got to the two red gas pumps. He clumped up the porch steps and sat down. His mother came out of the store.

"Is that you, Johnny?" she asked. "I thought you'd be later. Did you have a nice game?"

"No," said Johnny. "The kids in this place don't play ball."

"Oh, come," said his mother. "That can't be possible."

"Well, it is," said Johnny. "They have no place to play and they don't care whether they play or not. I invited them out here, and they wouldn't come." He pounded his fist into his glove.

His mother went back inside and soon came out with a glass of milk and a sandwich and two cookies on a plate.

"You'll feel better after you've had something to eat," she said. "By the way, Dad had to go over the hill for some seed corn and I'm looking after the store. Now that you're home, I'd be glad if you would take care of the gas pumps for me."

"All right," said Johnny, gloomily.

He *was* hungry, but it was silly to say that food would fix everything. He sat on the porch and ate his sandwich and stared at the two red gas pumps by the road. His father had showed him how to work them and how to put gasoline into the cars. Usually it was a treat to be allowed to do it. But today it was just something he might as well do because he had nothing else to do.

A few people came from down the road to buy groceries. Johnny idly listened to them talking to his mother, saying what a nice day it was. They said it was about time we had some good weather, after all that rain.

By and by a car, coming out from town, stopped in front of the first pump. Its horn tooted. Johnny looked up. It was a jeep, painted red. Johnny got up and clumped slowly down the steps. Probably one of the boys from the college. Lots of them had jeeps.

In the jeep sat a young man and a dog. The young man had curly brown hair and freckles. He wore a white sweater with a big H on the front. H for Hollister.

The dog had curly brown hair, too, but, of course, no sweater telling where he came from. In fact, you couldn't even tell what family of dogs he came from. One ear stood up and the other drooped over, and his whiskers stuck out all around his mouth. He looked a little like an airedale but he had a long, bushy tail!

"Hello, Chief," said the young man to Johnny. "Can I get some gas?"

Johnny didn't answer. He had caught sight of something in the back of the jeep. A baseball mitt and three bats! Why, this young man must be on the baseball team! Wow!

"Excuse me," said the young man, "but do you think I could get some gas?"

Johnny didn't hear a word. "Mister," he said, "do you play baseball?"

"Sure," said the young man. "Do you?"

"You bet I do," answered Johnny, grinning. "That is, I would if I had a chance."

"I'm sure you would," said the young man, "but about that gas—"

But Johnny just *had* to ask some more questions. "Do you play for the college?"

"Yes, sir," said the young man.

"You do!" exclaimed Johnny. "Would you mind telling me your name?"

"Andrew Jackson Sedgwick," said the young man.

Andrew Jackson! The name seemed familiar to Johnny. He was sure he had heard it before but he couldn't think where.

"Mine is Johnny Burton," he said. "Are you on the team?"

"Yes. I tried out today and I made it. And you know what that means?"

"Sure," said Johnny. "You're awful lucky."

The young man pretended to be insulted. "That's a fine thing to say to a baseball player! Don't you know you must never use the word lucky?"

"I—I didn't mean you were a lucky player," said Johnny. "I just meant you were lucky to be able to play. I wish *I* could."

"Well, can't you?"

"No," said Johnny. "The kids don't want to play. They say they have no place to play. It certainly is funny, way off here in the country."

The young man had such a nice face and he looked so interested, that before Johnny knew it he was telling him about everything that had happened that day.

The young man nodded sympathetically.

"It does seem as if something ought to be done," he said.

"What could we do, Mr. Sedgwick?" Johnny asked.

"Just call me Jackson," said the young man. "Never mind the Mister Sedgwick. I don't know right now what you might do. I'll give the matter my attention. But I asked you before if you knew what it means to be on the team. It means I have to study extra hard. You can't stay on the team if you don't get good marks. So I'd like to get some gas so that I can get home. Otherwise, I might have to stay here. Is your father around?"

"Oh, I can give you the gas all right," said Johnny. He reached up for the nozzle and unscrewed the cap of the jeep's gas tank. He set the pump going.

"I'll take five," said Jackson. "Say, you're a smart young fellow. Big help to your father, I'll bet."

"Yes," said Johnny. He was trying to think of some way to keep Jackson there talking a little longer. *Ding, ding, ding, ding, ding,* went the pump. Five gallons. Johnny put the nozzle back, took the money, screwed on the cap.

"What position do you play?" he asked.

"First base," said Jackson. "Now I'd better be getting home. I've got to help *my* father."

"*Your* father?" Johnny asked.

"Yes. He's a professor at the college. He's writing a book and I have to help him with the research."

"What position do you play?" Johnny asked. "First base," said Jackson

"What's it about?" Johnny asked, not because he was very interested but because he wanted to keep on asking questions.

"It's a history—" Jackson began.

"Oh! History!" said Johnny. He didn't want to hear any more about history. It seemed that he was getting an awfully big dose of history today.

Jackson laughed. "What's the matter? Don't you like history?"

"Well, it's—it's all right, I guess," said Johnny, not wanting to offend Jackson. "Only there's too many Indians in it. I guess that's why the kids around here play Indians so much instead of something sensible."

"I see," said Jackson. "Well, I don't think history should interfere with baseball. My father thinks so, though."

"He does!" said Johnny, indignantly.

"Yes. He doesn't see any more sense in baseball than you do in history. He doesn't think I ought to waste my time on the team."

Johnny sputtered, "B—but why—?"

"I don't know," said Jackson, "but he doesn't. So I'll have to get home and do my work or he'll be quite annoyed and make me get off the team. Goodbye." And he turned the key in the switch and prepared to drive away, leaving Johnny fuming with indignation.

But he didn't drive away. At that moment a gray cat came around the corner of the house and down the brick path. Jackson saw him and asked, "Is that your cat?"

"Yes," said Johnny, eagerly, seeing another way to keep the conversation going. "His name is Ted Williams. We call him that because he used to bat at things when he was a kitten."

Just then the brown dog, which had been sitting quietly in the jeep all this time, saw the cat, too. He gave a bark and leaped out of the jeep. The cat bounced around. His back went up and his tail fuzzed and he gave one loud hiss. Then he ran, and the dog ran after him.

"Come here!" Jackson shouted. "Daniel! Come back here!"

But Daniel paid no attention. Barking happily, he chased the cat across the road, over the wooden bridge and behind the little stone house. A minute later there was a crash, as if a rock had fallen.

Jackson jumped out of the jeep and ran, and Johnny ran after him, over the bridge and behind the house. There they stopped and looked around. The cat was nowhere in sight. He had disappeared. Only the dog was there, jumping up and down and barking at the willow tree.

"Where's that cat?" Jackson demanded.

"Maybe he's up in the tree," said Johnny.

They peered up in the willow, but the cat was not visible.

"He could have run up the tree and onto the roof of the house," said Jackson. But he wasn't on the roof.

"Something fell," said Johnny. "I heard it."

"It couldn't have been the cat," said Jackson. "It sounded like a rock. But I don't see any fallen rock."

"Neither do I," said Johnny.

"Well, Daniel Boone," said Jackson to his dog, "you come here. You've caused enough trouble."

But the dog pretended not to hear a word. He wanted to get that cat, wherever it was. He kept on jumping at the tree. He made a great leap and fell in the brook.

"Oh, drat that dog!" said Jackson. He reached down the bank and pulled his pet out by the collar. The dog shook himself. Muddy water flew in all directions.

"Now I've got to ride home with him," said Jackson. "He's all wet. And when he's wet he smells. Smell him?"

Johnny chuckled. "I sure do. What is it?"

"He chased a skunk. He's an explorer. That's why I call him Daniel Boone. He explored right in the skunk's nest."

"I'm sorry my cat came along just then," said Johnny.

"It's not your fault. It's mine for not tying Daniel up. He chased after me when I started for college this morning, and I didn't see him till I was halfway there, and then I couldn't go back so I took him with me. He's been in college all day and now he wants to play."

He started back across the bridge, dragging the dog by the collar. But suddenly he turned and looked back at the field.

"Say, Johnny!" he exclaimed. "What do you mean, no place to play? This field would be perfect!"

"Sure," said Johnny. "I know it would. But the kids won't come out here. They don't want to walk four miles."

"That's too bad," said Jackson.

He stood there, looking at Johnny and at the

field. And then an idea struck him. Johnny could see it in his face.

"I have it!" he said. "I can help you out."

"How?" Johnny asked.

"Well, I'll tell you," said Jackson. "I come out this way every day about half-past three. I could bring some kids out with me in the jeep. Think they'd like that?"

"Would they!" Johnny yelled. "Yowee!" And he began to do an Indian war dance right there on the bridge.

"Hey, watch out!" said Jackson. "I don't want to have to pull you out of the brook, too. Daniel Boone is enough."

"Well, gosh, it's awfully nice of you," said Johnny. "Just wait till I tell the fellows."

"That's to make up for Daniel Boone chasing your cat," said Jackson. He got into his jeep and stepped on the starter. Daniel Boone jumped in beside him, but Jackson picked him up and dumped him in the back.

"You smell," he said. "OK, Johnny, you and the boys meet me at the college gate tomorrow at three-thirty."

The jeep roared away in a cloud of dust.

Johnny stood by the pump, watching the little red car disappear in the distance.

"Jumping grasshoppers!" he said to himself. "We're going to play ball, after all. What a nice guy!"

4. The First Practice

AT SUPPER that night Johnny was so excited that he could hardly eat. He kept talking about Jackson and the jeep, baseball and Daniel Boone.

"What a funny name for a dog!" his mother said.

"Jackson said the dog was an explorer," Johnny said. "Last week he explored a skunk's nest."

"Oh, I see," said his mother, laughing.

Johnny was glad she saw and wasn't going to ask him any more questions. He himself couldn't quite remember just what Daniel Boone had explored. He was on the point of asking, when it occurred to him that perhaps he had better not get his parents

started on history. He had had enough history for one day. Maybe he'd better look up Daniel Boone in his book.

"Maybe Jackson thought Ted Williams was a funny name for a cat," he said.

Ted Williams, hearing his name called, got up from his seat in the corner and came and rubbed his head against Johnny's knee.

"Where did you disappear to this afternoon?" Johnny asked.

Ted Williams did not answer. He went back to his corner and sat down again.

"You better watch out," Johnny told him. "Tomorrow a bunch of us will arrive in the jeep, and if that dog is there, he'll chase you again."

"Before you ride in the jeep," his father said, "I'd like to find out a little more about the dog's master. He may be a fine young man, but we don't know him and we can't have you riding in jeeps with anybody we don't know."

Johnny stared in surprise. "But Pop!" he exclaimed. "He's at the college! I saw the H on his sweater!"

"That doesn't make him a safe driver," said his father. "We don't even know his whole name."

"I do so," said Johnny, indignantly. "It's Andrew Jackson Sedgwick. His father is a professor or something."

"Sedgwick!" said Mr. Burton. "A professor? Why, Sedgwick is the name of the man I bought the seed corn from. But he's a farmer. Maybe he's some relation."

"Call him up, Pop," said Johnny. "Quick, call him up and ask him. Jackson said he lived over the hill. Go on, call him up now."

Mr. Burton went to the telephone. Pretty soon he came back, smiling.

"Well, is he any relation to Jackson?" Johnny asked.

"Yes, quite a close relation," said Mr. Burton. "He's his father."

"But is Mr. Sedgwick a professor?" Johnny asked.

"It seems so," his father answered. "But he's a farmer, too. I don't know how he gets time for both."

"I guess that's why Jackson has to help him with his book," said Johnny.

"What's the book about?" his mother asked.

"It's about history," Johnny said. "But I don't know what kind. We were mostly talking about baseball. Well, Pop, is it all right for us to ride with him in the jeep?"

"Yes," said his father, "so long as you don't fall out. Mr. Sedgwick says his son is a good driver."

Johnny went to bed early that night. He wanted to get up in time for a little catching practice in the morning so as to make a good showing the next afternoon, and he wanted to be by himself to decide how to persuade the boys to come.

But it turned out that they didn't need very much persuading. They were quite willing to come if they could have a ride in a jeep. They were even willing to walk the two miles back to town.

At half-past three all six of them were waiting at

"Hi, Jackson!" Johnny yelled. "That was some catch!"

the college gates. A red jeep stood by the curb, but Jackson was not there. Through the iron bars of the fence they could see the college baseball diamond, where a practice game was going on. As they watched, a man came up to bat. He was a big man. Even through the fence the boys could see that he looked like a good hitter. The pitch came, and the big batter swung. They could hear the loud "plunk" as his bat hit the ball and sent it sailing.

"It's a homer!" Johnny said. And it certainly looked like it. But somebody was running. It was one of the outfielders. Watching the ball, he galloped along under it and then, almost falling into the wooden grandstand, he snatched it out of the air. A cheer went up from the players. Apparently that was the third out of the game, for the men began coming in from the outfield.

"Boy, that was some catch!" Johnny said to the boys. "Did you see how he ran under it?"

The men were jogging off to the field house. All but one—the one who had made the catch. He came toward them. It was Jackson.

"Hi, Jackson!" Johnny yelled. "That was some catch! Boy, that was wonderful!"

Jackson grinned. "Glad you liked it," he said.

"Just wait here. I'll be right with you." And he trotted off.

Johnny sighed. It was wonderful to know a man like that.

"Isn't he swell!" he exclaimed.

Max nodded. "But I do not think we shall be able to play so good like that," he said, doubtfully.

"Oh, sure we will," said Joe. "I'll ask my brother and he'll show me the good plays, and then we'll be all right. We're out of practice right now. But just wait."

Johnny was surprised. He didn't think they had had *any* practice. But he said nothing.

Pretty soon Jackson came trotting back across the grass and with him, barking and leaping, was Daniel Boone.

"I thought you were going to leave him at home," Johnny said.

Jackson laughed. "I tried to," he said. "I tied him up. But he must have chewed the rope. When I was halfway to town, there he was, running along the road. So I had to let him come."

He looked around at the boys. "Hello, fellows," he said.

"Hello, Mr. Jackson," the boys answered.

"Climb in," said Jackson. "Johnny, you hold Daniel Boone on your lap. And everybody hold on tight. Don't fall out."

The wind blew all around them. The houses and trees whizzed past. It was much more fun than riding in the bus, which bumbled along and had to keep stopping to let people off.

In a few minutes they were there. The boys jumped down. Daniel Boone jumped down, too, and sniffed around.

"He's looking for my cat," said Johnny.

"Catch him," said Jackson. "Hurry up, before he gets away." Johnny grabbed Daniel Boone and dumped him in the jeep.

"Can't you stay a while?" he asked. But Jackson shook his head.

"Sorry. I have to study today." He put his foot on the gas pedal, waved his hand at the boys and drove off. Daniel Boone looked back at them over the edge of the jeep, as if he would have liked to stay.

"Well, come on," said Johnny, when the jeep was out of sight. "Come up to the house. I'll just get my stuff and be right out."

He ran up the stairs two at a time. When he came

down, his mother was out on the porch, talking to the boys.

"Hello, dear," she said. "I was just telling the boys that when you get through playing I'll have some refreshments for you."

"Thank you, Mom," said Johnny. "Come on, gang, let's go."

But Howard said, "Could we have just a drink of water now?"

"Hey, you don't want to drink water before you play," Johnny protested.

"Oh, just a little drink," said Howard.

Mrs. Burton brought glasses of water and they all had drinks, except Johnny.

Then he led the boys across the road. He wanted to get started. But the boys were in no hurry. They looked around at everything.

"This is a pretty good place," said Joe. "Can you work those gas pumps?"

"Yes," said Johnny. "Some time I'll show you. But now let's play ball."

They crossed the road and the boys stopped to examine the little stone house. Buster was interested in it.

"What's in here?" he asked.

"Nothing," said Johnny. "Just some boxes of canned goods my father keeps inside."

"I'd like to see," said Buster. "Is it locked? Couldn't you get the key from your father?"

"Maybe I will some time," said Johnny. He dragged them away from the house and across the bridge. Now they got interested in the brook.

"This is swell," said Howard. "I bet we could fish here."

"No, there aren't any fish," said Johnny.

But Howard insisted on getting down on his stomach, and his twin brother followed suit.

"There's a snake!" they both yelled. They jumped down off the bridge and the other boys followed. The snake got away, but Charles caught a little frog and they had to take turns holding it. At last the frog got away, too. The boys climbed out of the brook bed and took a look at the back of the stone house.

"Look at that!" Buster exclaimed. "A door that opens over the brook! What's the idea?"

"I don't know," said Johnny. "That's how they built it. Only it doesn't open."

"It must be real old," said Buster. "How old do you guess it is?"

"I don't know," said Johnny. "Come on. Let's play ball."

"I bet it's a hundred years old," said Buster.

"I bet there were Indians here when that was built," said Joe.

At the word "Indians," Howard began to run around in a circle, shouting, "Wah-wah-wah-wah!"

"Let's play Indians," said Charles.

"No," said Johnny, firmly. "We came here to play baseball. Come on."

At last the boys followed him out to the field. They looked all around.

Joe approved. "This is a good field," he said. "It's better than that lot on Oak Street. Wait till I tell my brother. I bet when we get real good we'll be able to lick those guys."

"Well, how about getting started then?" suggested Johnny. He was getting tired of reminding them. "Look. Here's a flat rock. This can be home plate. We'd better just have one base today. You want me to pitch?"

"Sure," said Buster. "Let Joe pitch for the other side."

"Yeah, I'll pitch; my brother showed me how," said Joe.

Johnny chose Buster and Howard for his side, and Joe took Charles and Max. Johnny looked around for something to serve as first base.

"That tree stump over there is good," he said, pointing to a big flat stump that looked as if it had been dead a long time.

He took his position about twenty feet away from home plate. Buster took first base and Howard prepared to catch, while Joe took up the bat and stood ready for the pitch. Johnny let go with a nice fast ball. Joe chopped at it, but he didn't come near hitting it. It sailed past Howard and rolled toward the brook.

"Get it before it gets wet!" Johnny shouted. But Howard couldn't run fast enough. The ball rolled down the bank into the water. Howard scrambled down and came back wiping it on his pants.

"I'm sorry," he said. "But you threw so hard!"

Johnny was surprised. That was not what he would have called a very hard ball. He decided to make the next one easy. But Joe couldn't reach that either. This time, however, Howard stopped it before it got to the brook and threw it to Johnny. It fell about six feet short of him.

"Hey, what's the matter with you guys?" Johnny called.

"We're out of practice," said Joe. "Come on, give us a good ball for a change."

"There was nothing the matter with the first two," Johnny said. But he pitched again.

This time Joe hit the ball. He flung his bat away and galloped to first base. Howard picked up the ball and started to run after him with it.

"Throw it!" Johnny yelled. "Throw it to Buster!"

Howard threw, but too far. The ball went way beyond the stump. Buster had to turn and run after it, and in the meantime Joe touched base and galloped home again.

"We got a run! We got a run!" he yelled, jumping up and down.

Max and Charles jumped and yelled, too.

Johnny said, "Well, it isn't much to get a run out of that kind of playing."

"Aw, you're sore because we got a run," Joe said. "Boy! This is fun. Come on, Max, you're up next."

Max timidly took the bat. "I don't know if I can hit," he said, meekly.

"That's all right, Maxie," said Johnny. "You do the best you can."

Max gripped the bat. He frowned.

"All right," he announced. "Now am I ready."

Johnny pitched a very slow, easy ball. Max just stood there. When the ball went past him he turned around to look after it.

"What's the matter?" Johnny asked.

Max said, "I am holding the bat, but you do not hit it. Maybe I don't hold it right."

"Oh! Jumping grasshoppers!" said Johnny. "He expects me to hit the bat with the ball!"

The boys couldn't help laughing. Max laughed, too, good-naturedly.

"I did not do right?" he asked. "Chonny, I tell you what. You hit the ball. I will watch you."

Johnny took the bat. Joe pitched. He wound up as if he had been Bob Feller. Then he threw. Johnny swung back and hit with all his might. The ball sailed through the air while Johnny galloped to first base and back.

"That was wonderful!" said Max. "Now I do the same."

"Sure!" said Johnny. "Where's the ball?"

"It went over past the stump," said Charles. He

looked around in the grass, but the ball wasn't there.

The other boys came and looked. They beat the ground with the bat and walked all around, but the ball had disappeared. What could have happened to it?

"Oh, shucks," said Johnny. "It was a good ball, too. And now how can we play?"

"Golly, that's too bad," said Buster. "Look, Johnny, I've got a ball at home. I'll bring it tomorrow and you can have it."

"Yes, that's a good idea," said Howard. "And now let's play Indians."

5. Jackson to the Rescue

JOHNNY didn't know what to do. He had thought his problem was solved. He had thought that if he could just get the boys to come out and start playing, they would like it so much that they would go ahead and play. And they hadn't. First they had fooled around, poking in the brook, examining the little stone house. Then they had lost the ball, just because Charles couldn't keep his eye on it. Then they had spent the rest of the afternoon playing Indians. It was true that it had been fun. Even Johnny had had fun, hiding behind trees and leaping out with loud war whoops to scalp the poor settlers. But it wasn't baseball.

The boys had eaten cookies and they had watched

Mr. Burton work on a car, and then a farmer had come along in a truck and given them a ride home. They had gone off happily, shouting back to Johnny about what a good time they had had.

Now Johnny sat at his desk, with his book open in front of him. Ted Williams lay asleep in his lap. Johnny smoothed Ted's whiskers. His eyes were on the page but they didn't see what was printed there. He was too busy with his thoughts. He knew he ought to be studying. They were going to have a test tomorrow. It was going to be about the pioneers.

"Let's see," said Johnny, looking at the map. "We've got to know how the pioneers came here. Some of them came through the Cumberland Gap, across Kentucky and down the Ohio River." He turned a page. There was a picture of a tall man, leading a horse on which a woman was riding. The caption said, "Daniel Boone, leading a party through the Cumberland Gap."

"Daniel Boone!" Johnny exclaimed. "Sure enough! He explored Kentucky!"

He went back to the map. "Others came across Pennsylvania to Pittsburgh and down the Ohio River." Johnny sighed. Jumping grasshoppers!

What did he care about how they got to the Ohio River? He wanted to play baseball. What good was an education if it didn't solve his problems? He turned some more pages.

Suddenly his eye lit on a picture of another man. He was a funny-looking man. His hair stuck straight up in the air and he looked very solemn. Underneath it said, "Andrew Jackson, elected President in 1828."

Andrew Jackson! So *that* was the man Jackson was named for! Of course! His father was a history professor, so he called his son Andrew Jackson! Johnny laughed. Well, maybe history was some use, after all. It hadn't exactly solved his problem but it had given him an idea what to do about it. He would speak to Jackson. Maybe Jackson could help him.

The main thing was to figure out how to speak to Jackson alone. But that turned out to be easy, too. The boys were all ready to start at three o'clock the next day, when Buster remembered that he had left his ball at home.

"OK," said Johnny, "you go back for it and I'll run ahead and tell Jackson you're coming, and the other guys can take their time."

He ran as fast as he could. Jackson was at the gates. He didn't have his uniform on today. Daniel Boone ran up to welcome Johnny. He waved his tail and grinned, with his tongue hanging out.

"I just can't keep that dog at home," Jackson explained.

"Did you tie him up?" Johnny asked.

"Yes," said Jackson. "But I think he knows how to untie knots. Well, how did it go yesterday? Have a good game?"

Johnny shook his head sadly. "No. The guys fooled around, and then we lost the ball."

"Lost the ball!" said Jackson. "That's too bad."

"Well, I can get another ball, I guess," said Johnny. "But the worst thing is that they don't care about playing, and I can't make them."

"You can't?"

"No. I tell them to come on, and they don't pay any attention. I can't get them interested."

Jackson didn't answer for a minute. He stood looking thoughtfully at Johnny. Then his face got all bright, the way it had the other day when he thought of driving the boys out to Johnny's house.

"What do you think?" he asked. "Think they'd like to watch the college team play for a while? That might get their interest up."

"You bet it would!" exclaimed Johnny. "Golly, Jackson, I knew you'd think of something."

"All right, wait here," said Jackson. "I'll be right back."

He ran across the grass to speak to the coach. Soon he was back, just as the boys came marching along the street.

"Come on, everybody," he said. "We're going to see the end of the game."

He led the boys to the front row of the wooden grandstand. The sun shone brightly on the green diamond and the men in their gray practice uniforms.

"Now, boys," said Jackson, "keep your eyes on the fellow that's up at bat. That's McGillicuddy, our star hitter."

A thin, rangy fellow was standing at the plate, waiting for the pitch. When it came, it was way outside. The batter didn't move.

"Ball one," said the umpire.

"It looks as if they were going to walk him," said Jackson. "We're ahead three to two and they don't want McGillicuddy to hit a home run with the bases full."

Jackson led the boys to the front row of the wooden grandstand

"But if they walk him," Max asked, "what will happen? Will they have two men on one base?"

"No." Jackson laughed. "Everybody will advance one base and the man on third will get home."

"Then will the score be four to two?" asked Max.

"Right," said Jackson. "But if this slugger hits a home run, he'll drive in all three men, and that will make it seven to two."

"Oh," said Max. "I understand. Soon I learn a lot about baseball."

"Yeah," said Joe. "Pretty soon we'll get so good we'll—"

"Wait a minute," said Jackson. "You'll get good faster if you watch these fellows."

The umpire had called, "Ball two" and "Ball three." They were waiting for ball four. But the fourth one slipped somehow. It went right across the center of the plate. The batter was on his toes. He swung at it and knocked it into the grandstand on the other side of the field. A cheer went up from the team. The three base runners scored. The batter trotted around the bases and then grinned up at the boys and tipped his cap to them.

Johnny sighed. He wished he were grown up and could play ball as much as he liked. He'd get on that team. He could see himself down there at the plate, swinging the way McGillicuddy had done and then trotting around the bases, the crowd cheering and the coaches patting him on the back as he went by.

Coaches! If only they had a coach now! Another idea came into his head. He turned and looked at Jackson. He didn't feel quite brave enough to say what he was thinking. And then suddenly it slipped out.

"Jackson," he asked, "would you coach us?"

"Would I *what?*" said Jackson.

Johnny's face grew red. "I said, would—would you c-coach us a little, I mean, you know, I just mean—" He got all tangled up and stopped.

Jackson grinned at him. "Didn't I tell you how much I have to study?" he asked.

"Sure," said Johnny, "but you could maybe stay for half an hour and sort of show us a few things. Would you?" He looked earnestly up at Jackson. "You know, a little fresh air and exercise would do you good."

Jackson burst out laughing. "It's nice of you to think of my health," he said. "Well, I'll think about it."

Johnny didn't know what that meant—whether

he'd have to think for a couple of days or a week. All the way home Jackson didn't say another word about it, and Johnny was too busy balancing Daniel Boone on his lap to ask him. But when they arrived at the two red gas pumps, instead of just stopping to let the boys out, Jackson ran the jeep off the road into the parking space and turned off the motor.

"Are you going to stay?" Johnny asked, not quite believing in his good luck.

"Well, this is Friday," said Jackson, "so I don't have to study so much tonight. I'll stay a while and watch you."

"You will!" exclaimed Johnny. "Oh, boy! That's swell! Hey, fellows, Jackson is going to stay and watch us!"

The boys were just as pleased as Johnny. They liked Jackson.

"We're a little out of practice," said Joe. "But after a while we'll get pretty good."

They waited for Johnny to get his equipment, and then they went out to the field. Daniel Boone ran around in circles, sniffing the grass. Jackson walked across the field and sat down on the big stump.

"That's our first base," said Johnny.

"That's all right," Jackson called. "I'll duck when

the ball comes my way."

"OK, guys," said Johnny, "let's have the same line-up as yesterday. Let's show Jackson what we can do."

"You bet," said Joe, walking to the pitcher's box. "We'll show him."

Max stood behind the plate to catch, and Howard moved over to the stump to cover first.

Johnny picked up the bat. Now was his chance to show Jackson something. Joe began to pitch. He threw too high, too low, too short, too wide. And Max couldn't catch. He had to run after half the balls.

Johnny waited and waited. Finally he swung, and the ball sailed through the air, right past Howard. Jackson jumped out of the way. Howard started to run after the ball, while Johnny trotted to first base and back. And again Buster and Charles began to shout, "We got a run! We got a run!"

"Oh, quiet!" said Johnny. "What's the good of a run like that?"

He gave the bat a kick. He just couldn't help it.

Jackson got up from the stump and walked to the plate.

"Now, boys," he said, "you're all pretty good, but

you need some pointers."

Joe said, "Well, I pitched and pitched, but Johnny didn't hit."

"You did not throw straight," said Max. "All the time I have to run after the ball."

"You can't catch," said Joe.

"Now, listen," said Jackson, "the best ball players need practice. Do you think they just go out and play games? No, sir. They practice."

"Well, how should we practice?" Joe asked. "My brother doesn't practice. He goes right out and plays."

"I bet your brother has plenty of practice," said Jackson. "Doesn't he play catch a lot?"

"Sure," said Joe.

"Well, that's practice," said Jackson. "Now here's what you do. Get in two lines, facing each other."

The boys lined up.

"Now, Johnny, you stand out here and throw me the ball, and the rest watch what I do."

Johnny threw and Jackson reached up and caught the ball with his left hand and covered it with his right. Then he threw to Johnny. He put the ball right into Johnny's hands.

"You must keep your eye on the ball every min-

ute," he said. "And you must learn to aim. A pitcher must know what spot in the air he's aiming to hit. And that goes for the others, too. If you're throwing to another player, put the ball where he can reach it. And, Max, put some power into your throw. You've got a good, strong right arm there."

"Excuse me," said Max, "but my right arm is not so good. Would it be all right if I throw with my left arm?"

"Left arm! A southpaw!" said Jackson. "Of course."

"I did not know," said Max. "I see everybody throwing with their right arm. I think I must do the same."

"Now," said Jackson, "we'll have throwing and catching practice. Back and forth, from one line to the other."

The boys practiced for about ten minutes. At first the ball fell on the ground quite a lot. But soon they began to hold on to it. Now Jackson had them stand farther apart.

They began to get some rhythm into it. *Pock, pock, pock, pock,* the ball went.

"Golly, we're getting good," said Buster.

"You bet," said Joe. "Wait till I tell my brother."

"You and your brother," said Howard.

"Better stop and rest a while," said Jackson. "Everybody sit down, and Joe will tell us about his brother."

For once Joe had nothing to say. He grinned, but his face got a little red and he kept quiet.

Johnny gazed at Jackson with admiration. "It's awfully nice of you to help us out," he said. "Would you mind if we called you Coach?"

Jackson picked a grass blade and chewed it. Then he said, "No, I wouldn't mind. I'd like it. But you know I can't promise to come every day. I have so much work—"

"We know about that," said Johnny.

"But I'll come when I can," said Jackson. "I like coaching. I think it's a good idea." He jumped up. "Now, boys," he said, "we'll have a little batting practice. You line up and I'll pitch to you. Who knows where the pitch has to be?"

Joe shouted, "Between the knee and the shoulder.

My brother—" but he didn't finish.

Max took the bat first. He grasped it tightly around the middle and stood with his feet close together, tensely waiting.

Jackson waved his arm. "Relax, Max," he said. "Put the bat down and shake your arms. That's it. As if they were rags. Now face the other way, since you're lefty. Put your feet apart to balance you, and hold the bat farther down. Not so tight. It won't get away from you. Now, here goes."

Max swung back, and as the ball came he swung forward and hit it hard. He looked around, worried; then it came to him that he had hit the ball.

"I hit it! I hit!" he yelled.

The others thumped him on the back.

"Babe Ruth Schlussel!" said Johnny.

Now the others had their turns. Jackson was a good pitcher. He could put the ball exactly where he wanted it.

At last he said, "OK, boys, that's all for today. Got to go now."

They walked to the jeep with him and watched as he climbed in and Daniel Boone jumped in beside him. Jackson waved, started the motor and drove off.

The boys turned and looked at each other and grinned. Johnny grinned the widest of all.

"What do you know!" he said. "We've got a coach!"

6.

The Little Stone House

TED WILLIAMS, the cat, walked across the little bridge and out into the field behind the little old store building. He walked slowly, looking around, his tail switching now and then. The field had once been a good hunting ground, with plenty of field mice in the long grass. But now, ever since Johnny and those other boys had started running around like mad, hitting a round thing with a stick and flattening out the grass with their big feet, the field was spoiled. They had been coming every day for three weeks, and the mice had gone somewhere else.

And to make matters worse, the boys always brought that disgusting dog along. He seemed to think he was there for the purpose of hunting Ted Williams himself! It was a lucky thing that Ted knew how to get away or that dog would be chasing him across the field every day.

Quietly Ted picked his way across the field, past the old tree stump. The ground sloped a little here, and the grass was thicker and greener, showing that water sometimes stayed here after a rain. Ted walked on, through the waving grass that came about as high as his ears. He twitched his ears. The grass tickled them. His tail waved in the air.

Now he came to a little hole in the ground, hidden by the grass. In front of this hole he sat down and waited. His tail flicked. His green eyes watched. In the past he had seen rabbits coming out of this hole. But for some time now he had not seen any. They had probably gone somewhere else, too, like the mice. Still, it wouldn't hurt to watch for a while.

Suddenly, the quiet was broken by the rattle of machinery and the shouting of voices and the barking of a dog. There they were!

Ted Williams got up and started for the woods. There was no doubt about it. The place was spoiled.

The boys galloped across the bridge. It was Friday again. This was the day they were to have a game. Jackson had said so. On other days they had come out and practiced their catching and throwing, and batting and running. Jackson had waited for them to get started, and then, after half an hour or so, he had had to leave—he had so much studying to do—and they had gone on by themselves. But now it was Friday and he could stay longer.

Daniel Boone tore after the boys and dashed around in a circle as usual. Jackson often explained that when he left for college in the morning, he tied Daniel Boone up but somehow Daniel always got loose and followed him. After a day at college the dog had to let off steam.

Now he barked and ran around with his ears flapping, until he was tired. Then he sat down and panted. Then he got up and began to follow a trail through the grass. He ran past the stump and suddenly stopped and began to dig. The dirt flew out behind him. He snorted through his nose and dug some more.

"Hey, he's digging up the field!" Buster cried.

"Daniel!" Jackson commanded sternly. "Come here and sit down!"

Daniel came, regretfully, his nose covered with dirt.

Jackson looked up at the sky. "Better get going, boys," he said. "It looks like rain."

"What!" said Johnny. The sky was blue. Big white clouds hurried across it, but they didn't look like rain clouds.

"Can't tell in spring," said Jackson. "Warm up first."

The boys lined up for catching. They were getting pretty good. Every day they liked it more.

"Why didn't we ever do this before?" Buster inquired.

"We had no place to play," said Joe.

"And we had no coach," Charles added.

"I guess it's because we didn't have Johnny," Max said.

"Well, come on," said Jackson. "You can throw the bouquets later. Now let's throw the ball. Keep the teams the way they were. Johnny, Buster and Howard on one side. Joe, Max and Charles on the other. I'll pitch for both sides."

Now that they had Jackson to pitch, it was possible to have two bases.

Joe was up first. He was so eager to show how well he could hit that he whirled around without hitting anything. He did this three times and then threw the bat down in disgust.

"Your brother teach you that?" Buster yelled.

"Quiet!" said Joe, walking away from the plate.

Charles was next. He got to first base, and then Max was up.

Max gripped the bat tightly. He stood tense, waiting for the pitch. Jackson purposely threw him an easy ball. But he was too excited to swing. He pushed his bat at the ball and it fell to the ground in front of him. He looked up, embarrassed.

"Run!" everybody yelled. "It's a bunt! Go on, run!"

Max ran. He looked puzzled. When he got to first base he looked around. Howard, who was catching, had run forward, picked up the ball and thrown it to Johnny at first base, but not in time. Max was safe.

"Good for Max!" said Jackson.

"What did I do?" Max asked.

"You made a hit," Johnny told him.

"But what kind of a hit is that?" Max asked. "I did not swing."

"A bunt!" Johnny yelled. "You bunted. That's as good as a swing if it gets you to first base."

Max grinned. "Aha!" he said. "A bunt! All right, Charles, you make one, too."

"No!" Joe yelled. "Don't you know you mustn't tell the other team what you are going to do?"

Max stared at him. "No? Why not?"

"Ya dope! Then they'll get ready to put you out!"

"Aha!" said Max. "I see. In baseball, you have to fool the other fellows."

Charles didn't bunt. He got a hit, anyway, and put Max on second. Then Joe came up and struck out again.

"Now what do we do?" Charles asked. There was nobody to go to bat and get the other men home.

Johnny said, "The way we used to play, the man who struck out takes the place of the one on second base and that one goes to bat again."

Joe took Max's place, and Max went to bat with a grin on his face. He muttered, "Oh! Now better

I do not bunt again. They will expect me to bunt. Now will I swing!"

"Hey, quiet!" Joe shouted.

Max took the bat and waited for the pitch. When the ball came, he grinned and gently pushed the bat to meet it and it fell on the ground as before. Then he galloped for first base before Jim could recover from his surprise. Everybody laughed at his strategy.

"That's the way, Maxie, old boy," said Joe. "That's the way to fool 'em."

Max's hit brought Joe and Charles home. When Charles came to bat, he hit a pop fly into Johnny's hands, and that retired the side.

Now Johnny's team was up. Johnny looked at the sky. It didn't look so blue any more. The fluffy clouds had covered it all, and now they looked gray and threatening.

"Come on, guys," he said. "Let's get our innings before it starts to rain. Buster, you first."

Buster picked up his bat and stood waiting for the pitch. It came, but he let it go by. Another. And then a third.

"Hey, hurry up!" Johnny called to him. "We want a chance, too."

But as Buster stood there trying to decide to hit,

big drops began to fall. Buster took one big swing and connected. He began to run. Johnny and Howard cheered him home.

Johnny ran for the bat. But now the rain began to come down in earnest.

"Come on, kids," said Jackson. "Grab your gloves and let's go, before we get soaked."

They raced for the porch. Then they sat down and watched the rain. It was as if the sky had opened and tubs full of water were falling out. Drops splashed in the mud and bounced off the steps, and a sheet of water rolled off the roof and fell like a veil in front of them.

"Why couldn't it have waited till we got our innings?" Johnny demanded.

"Maybe we can play when it stops," said Joe.

Jackson shook his head. "Ground will be too wet."

Johnny's mother came out on the porch. "I heard somebody come up here," she said, "but I didn't know whether it was you or some customers."

"We're customers, Ma," said Johnny. "What have you got?"

"Nice fresh doughnuts," answered Mrs. Burton. "I'll get some."

She went inside and came back with a tray. The boys drank lemonade and ate doughnuts for a while in silence.

Suddenly Buster's eyes, gazing vaguely around at the wet landscape, came to rest on the little stone building across the road.

"Hey, Johnny," he said. "You told us you'd show us what's in that little house over there."

"That's right," said Joe. "What about it? Now we have nothing to do."

"That's the old store," said Johnny. "I told you once. There's nothing in it but a lot of groceries in boxes."

"You mean you have two stores?" Buster asked.

"No," said Johnny. "But that was the store they used a long time ago. Fifty years ago, I guess."

And then, to his surprise, Jackson said, "It's older than that, Johnny. That little house must be about a hundred and fifty years old."

Johnny stared at him. "Why, Jackson, how do you know?" he asked.

"I told you my father was a history professor," said Jackson. "He wrote a book about this part of the country, how it was settled." He laughed. "Let's see; that was two years ago. That was when I got that dog. My father was just writing about how Daniel Boone led the pioneers through the Cumberland Gap. So I decided to call my pup Daniel Boone. It's a good name. Where is he?"

He looked around. The dog was nowhere in sight. "Exploring, I guess," Jackson said.

"Is that house in the book?" Johnny asked.

"Well, no," said Jackson, "but Father had to study all the old houses in the neighborhood, so he found out about that one."

"Well, come on, let's see the house," Buster urged.

"OK, I'll ask Pop," said Johnny. He went inside. In a few minutes he was back. Mr. Burton was with him, carrying a key and a flashlight.

"Johnny says you boys want to see the inside of the old store," he said. "There isn't much to see, but come along."

He led the way across the road. The rain was letting up a bit now. The boys crowded into the doorway while Mr. Burton unlocked the door.

There was only one room in the little house.

It was dark inside and smelled musty and damp. The two little windows were so covered with dirt and cobwebs that hardly any light came through them. Mr. Burton flashed the beam around on the walls and floor.

"Aren't there any lights in here?" Buster asked.

"No," said Mr. Burton. "They didn't have electricity when this was built, and they never bothered to put it in. There's a kerosene lamp up there, though. I put it there so that I could see to work."

Jackson lit the little glass lamp. Its yellow light, reflected in the piece of tin behind it, threw queer shadows on the walls. Now that the boys could see better, they examined everything. Cartons of groceries stood all over the floor. The walls were lined with shelves. At one end of the room was a big fireplace. On either side of the fireplace were wooden pegs. There was a counter across the back of the room, and behind the counter was the big oak door over the brook.

Jackson was looking at the inside of the fireplace. "I was wondering," he said, "if we could make a fire. It would dry the place out."

"That's a good idea," said Mr. Burton. "The fireplace is all right, if that's what you were wondering about. Johnny, you and a couple of others go out and get some wood."

"How would you fellows like to use this place for a play house?"

Johnny, Max and Buster ran across the road, and came back with their arms full of firewood. Jackson laid the fire and lit it, and soon it blazed up bright and warm. The boys dragged boxes close to the hearth to sit on.

"Makes it nice and cheerful," said Mr. Burton. "They certainly knew how to build fireplaces in the old days. Well, have a good time, boys." He turned to go.

Then, with his hand on the doorknob, he stopped. "I just had an idea," he said. "How would you fellows like to use this place for a play house? I don't need it except to store extra canned goods."

The boys looked at each other as this idea took hold. Then they all nodded eagerly.

"You bet!" Buster said.

"That's a swell idea, Pop!" Johnny exclaimed.

"Can we leave our things here?" Joe asked.

"Of course," said Mr. Burton. "Only one thing. No fires unless a grownup is here."

"OK, Pop," said Johnny.

"Well, then, here's the key. You keep it. I have another one in the store." He handed Johnny the key and went out.

Buster said, "That was certainly nice of your father. We can have fun. Where should we keep the key?"

"We ought to have a special hiding place for it, that nobody knows about but us," said Johnny.

He looked around. Then he got up and opened the door and looked outside. He put his hand under the wooden step in front of the door.

"Look, fellows," he said. "There's a hole under here. This is where we'll keep it. Everybody see it?"

Everybody took notice of the hole. Johnny put the key in, came indoors and shut the door.

The boys went back to their seats around the fire.

Suddenly Johnny exclaimed, "Hey, fellows!"

Everybody stared at him.

"I've got a better idea than a play house. Why don't we have a club and use this for the club house?"

"What kind of a club?" Joe asked.

"A baseball club," said Johnny. "When Buster asked if we could leave our things here, that gave me the idea."

"It's a good idea," said Buster. "What'll we call it?"

They all tried to think of names, and stared at the

walls as if names might be written up there for them.

"We could hang the gloves on those pegs," said Howard, pointing to the wall beside the fireplace.

"That's right," said Johnny. "Say, Jackson, what are those for, anyhow?"

"They were for clothes," said Jackson. "They didn't have closets in the old days, you know."

"But this is a store," said Joe. "Why did they need closets in a store?"

"It was a house for people to live in before it was a store," Jackson answered. "I told you it was built about a hundred and fifty years ago."

"How did you find that out?" Buster asked.

"By the fireplace, for one thing," said Jackson. "The way it's built. It's made just like some of the oldest fireplaces in town. In fact, we think maybe the same person built all of them. You know there are some people that are very good at building fireplaces and chimneys."

"But wait a minute!" Buster broke in excitedly. "If this house is a hundred and fifty years old, that means it was built around 1800."

"About that," said Jackson. "1790, 1810—we can't tell exactly."

"But there were Indians around here then," said

Buster. "It was all woods. They built log houses, not stone houses. How could this have been built in 1800?"

"I see you know your history," Jackson said. "Well, that's why we're doubtful. It looks as if it was built then, and yet it doesn't seem possible."

"And if it was built around 1800," said Joe, "why was it built so far out of town, all by itself?"

Jackson shook his head. "I wish I knew," he said. "It's a mystery. If I knew the secret of this house, my life would be a lot easier." He yawned and stretched his long arms. "I wouldn't have so much work to do and I could stay and play with you kids a lot more."

"What do you mean, Jackson?" Johnny asked.

"I told you my father is working on a new book," said Jackson. "But I didn't tell you what it was about."

"What is it about?" asked Buster.

"It's a history of Willow Creek."

"You mean our town? The one we live in?"

"The same," said Jackson. "And it's a very hard job. That's why I have to help him."

The boys waited for him to go on. Why should it be such a hard job?

"Well, you know," said Jackson, "usually when you write a history of something, you find records. Either old letters, or books, or something that somebody wrote at the time, telling what they did. Then all you have to do is copy it down."

"Well, then," said Johnny, "why don't you copy down the Willow Creek records?"

"Because," said Jackson, "they only go back a hundred and fifty years, and before that there aren't any."

"But why should there be?" Buster asked. "If the town was started a hundred and fifty years ago, that's when the records ought to start."

"No," said Jackson. "They ought to go back farther. The people came from somewhere, didn't they?"

"Sure," said Johnny. "They came from back east somewhere."

"Well, we think they must have come down the Ohio River, as far as Cincinnati, and then up north. But there's nothing to say so. And there's nothing to say where they came from. The oldest book in the City Hall starts out like this: 'April 30, 1796. No news from Henry Totten. All quiet. Everybody busy. Building of new houses goes on.' "

"What does that mean? Who's Henry Totten?"

"Don't know," said Jackson. "Then later on it says something about somebody named Loomis 'going to Totten's house.' And again it says, 'No news from Henry Totten.'"

"Sounds as if Henry Totten had gone away from town," said Johnny. "Maybe he's the one who came way out here to build a house."

"We thought of that," said Jackson. "But then, why would they keep on saying 'No news from Totten'? And why was Totten so important? If he was just a man who wanted to get away from the rest and have a farm all by himself in the wilderness, why would they keep writing about him? And as Buster said, why would he build a stone house all by itself in the woods?"

Nobody could think of any answer to these questions. They all sat quietly, staring into the fire.

It was very strange. Johnny looked around at the room that he had been taking so much for granted. It was just a little old store, full of dust and boxes, and yet it was important enough to put in a history book. It had been here a hundred and fifty years ago, when the Indians were still nearby.

"Just think," he said to himself, "I might be sitting here and there would be woods all around. And suddenly I would hear—"

At that moment there was a scratching noise outside the door. Johnny jumped. Then he looked around to see if anybody had noticed. They hadn't. Johnny got up and opened the door. In rushed Daniel Boone, soaking wet and very muddy. He jumped on Jackson, lovingly wiping his dirty feet all over him. Then he shook himself hard, spraying water all over everybody.

"Hey, quit it!" Jackson yelled at him. "You're getting us all wet!"

Daniel Boone paid no attention. He gave himself a few more shakes and, after walking around in a circle four or five times, curled up in front of the fire. He gave a sigh, closed his eyes and went to sleep. The heat of the fire brought out the skunky smell of his fur.

"I don't know what I keep that dog for," said Jackson. "I don't know what use he is to anybody." He patted Daniel's rough fur.

"I know," said Johnny. "We could have him for a mascot for our club. Couldn't we, Jackson?"

"Of course, you can," said Jackson. "As long as you don't insist on keeping him here."

"I thought he was no use to you," said Johnny, laughing.

"He isn't," said Jackson, "but he'd get lonesome for me. And that gives me an idea for a name for the club. That is, if you want me to suggest one."

"Sure we do," said Buster.

"Well, since Daniel Boone was friendly with the Indians, you could call yourselves the Willow Creek Braves."

"That's a swell name," the boys agreed.

"This is wonderful," said Joe. "We have a club and a club house, and a coach and a mascot. We ought to be pretty good."

"Sure," said Buster. "All we need now is to learn how to play ball."

"I've got some rule books," Johnny said. "I'll bring them down and we can keep them on a shelf."

"We ought to clean it up a little," said Max. "There is plenty of dirt on the shelfs."

"OK," said Johnny. "I'll bring a broom and some rags. We can clean it up. And I've got some pennants in my room. I'll bring them, too."

"I've got a picture of Babe Ruth," said Howard. "I'll bring that."

The fire had burned low. Outside it was nearly

dark. Jackson looked at his watch.

"It's five o'clock," he said. "I've got to go. And how are you boys going to get home?"

"We'll get a lift," said Buster.

"Or Pop will drive them home," Johnny said.

"Well, then, somebody get a pail of water for the fire," said Jackson.

It seemed a shame to pour water on the glowing embers.

Johnny sighed a little. He could almost feel how it must have been in pioneer times, with the thick woods outside, and the stream bubbling past and perhaps a corn field planted where the baseball diamond was now. And inside everything snug and warm, with the firelight shining on the walls.

He poured the water on the hearth. A cloud of smoke and steam billowed up the chimney. Then Jackson blew out the lamp, and they went out into the rain.

7. A Key and a Book

IT RAINED all that week end. Johnny spent a large part of it staring out of the window. Part of the time he was looking at the sopping wet fields, wondering whether they could possibly be dry enough for baseball on Monday.

But part of the time he was looking across at the little stone house and thinking of what Jackson had said about it. It teased him. It was as if somebody had started to tell an exciting story and gone away without telling the end.

Johnny wanted to know the end. He kept thinking about Henry Totten. Who was Henry Totten, and why did he go away and where did he go?

By Sunday night Johnny had thought so much

about it that he had almost forgotten about baseball.

On Monday morning it was still raining. Well, they couldn't play that afternoon, he thought as he waited for the bus, with the rain dripping off his raincoat and sou'wester. But at least he would be able to talk to the boys about the club house.

The bus slowed down. Johnny jumped in and sat down, looking out at the gray sky and the dripping trees.

Suddenly he heard somebody in the back of the bus calling his name. "Hey, Johnny!"

He turned around. It was Michael Brown.

"I hear you kids are playing ball these aays," Michael said. The other big boys grinned and winked at each other. Johnny could see they were teasing him.

"Sure we are," he said. "You said I should play with somebody my size, remember?"

"Yes," said Michael, "and I hear the kids your size are pretty good."

Johnny was surprised. "Where'd you hear that?" he asked.

Michael didn't answer that. "I hear they're so good they can practically beat us already."

"I never said that," Johnny protested.

"Well, somebody did," said Michael. "We're real scared."

Johnny decided it was no use arguing, since he didn't know what Michael was talking about. He turned back and looked out of the window again.

When he got to school the boys were just as gloomy as the weather.

"Good weather for fishing," said Howard.

"Or frog hunting," said Charles.

"But not for ballplaying," said Max.

Joe said, "No. Too bad. We need to practice."

"I'll say we do," said Johnny. He was glad that Joe, who always knew everything, seemed to realize that they weren't big league players yet. And then suddenly that remark of Joe's seemed funny. There was something behind it.

"Say!" he said. "Who told Mike Brown we were playing ball?"

"I don't know," said Joe. "But maybe it was my brother. I told *him.*"

"What did you tell him?" Johnny asked.

Joe looked worried. "I was walking to school with him," he said. "And he was making fun of me. He said we were no good. So I said—well, I just said we were just as good as his gang. That's all."

Buster said doubtfully, "Are you sure that's all? You know, Joe, when you get to bragging—"

"Well, I can't remember what I said," Joe protested.

Johnny said, "Did you tell him anything about being good enough to beat them?"

"No. It wasn't me. It was my brother. He said we should prove it. And I said, sure. We'd prove it any time they liked."

Johnny groaned. So that was what Michael had meant.

"You sap," he said. "Now they'll make fun of us every time they see us."

"What'll we do?" Buster asked.

Johnny shook his head. Then he said, "There's only one thing to do now."

"What's that?" Howard asked.

"We've got to get so good that we can really play them," said Johnny. "We won't beat them. But at least we'll give them a good game. Then they'll have some respect for us."

Max was worried. "I do not play so good yet," he said. "I am afraid I will spoil the game."

"Don't be afraid, Maxie," said Johnny. "You'll be all right."

"But how can we get good enough?" Buster asked.

"Don't worry," said Johnny. "You do as I say and we'll be fine. It just means we've got to practice. We've got to practice every single day. We've got to have a team."

"But we only have six men," said Joe.

"Then we'll have a six-man team," said Johnny.

"All right, Johnny," said Buster. "You show us how and we'll do it."

"OK," said Johnny.

He felt full of confidence. Now the boys were really in earnest. He felt that nothing could stop them.

But that afternoon, when he came out of school and the rain drizzled down his neck, he didn't feel so sure. He walked to the bus. Michael Brown was sitting in the back seat already. Johnny felt less sure than ever.

And suddenly he thought of Jackson. He wanted to talk to Jackson about it. He turned around and walked quickly away from the bus. He splashed through the puddles as he ran along toward the college.

Then he heard someone calling, "Hey, Johnny! Wait for me!"

It was Buster.

His thin, serious face was screwed up into a scowl, and his glasses were wet with the rain.

"Wait a minute," he panted. "I'm coming with you."

"But it's raining," said Johnny. "We can't play."

"No," said Buster, "but I had another idea. You said you had some rule books. I thought maybe we could study the rules."

"Gee, that's a good idea," said Johnny. "OK, let's go."

Jackson's red jeep was at the curb and Jackson was in it, just starting the motor. The boys began to run.

Jackson was surprised to see them. "I didn't think you'd be coming today. I thought Johnny would be taking the bus."

"We had to see you," Johnny said. "We need your advice."

"All the advice you want, free of charge," said Jackson. "Climb in."

As they chugged along, Johnny explained their problem. "It's all because that Joe can't keep quiet," he said. "He said his brother was making fun of him, but I bet his brother wouldn't have said

As they chugged along, Johnny explained. "It's all because that Joe can't keep quiet," he said

a thing if he hadn't been boasting about us, just the way he boasts to us about his brother."

Jackson, keeping his eyes on the wet road ahead, nodded. "I think you're right, Johnny. So what do you want to do about it?"

"The only thing to do is practice till we get so good that we can play those guys. I don't say we'll ever beat them. But at least we'll give them some opposition."

"Well," said Jackson, "what's your plan?"

"We thought maybe you'd help us," said Johnny. "We thought if you could coach us a little more and we practiced every day, why then we might get pretty good—"

"I think you have the right idea, Johnny," Jackson said. "I know you will get pretty good."

His voice sounded odd as he said this. Johnny turned to look at him. There was something funny about his face. He seemed to be feeling badly about something.

"What's the matter, Jackson?" he asked, quickly.

"The trouble is," said Jackson, "that I won't be able to help you."

Johnny and Buster were startled. "Why not? What happened? Did we do something?"

"Calm yourselves," said Jackson. "It certainly isn't your fault. It's all on account of that book my father is writing."

Johnny slapped his wet raincoat in disgust. History was just a pain in the neck. He'd always thought so and this proved he was right.

"What has the book got to do with baseball?" he asked.

"It's like this," said Jackson. "You know that I'm helping my father with the book. Well, we haven't been able to find all the material we need to finish it. And it has to be finished in a hurry."

"Why?" Johnny asked.

"Well, the publishers are after my father," Jackson explained. "They say that if he can't finish the book this spring, they can't publish it at all."

"Why?" Johnny asked again.

"That's something I'd be glad if you would tell me," said Jackson. "But never mind. It has to be done. And I have to spend all my spare time doing research. I'll have to take a trip to Greenville. They may have books in the library there, that will help. So you see, I won't have much time. I'll even have to drop out of the college team."

Johnny and Buster both regarded him with horror. That was a real calamity. To get on the team and then have to drop out to read history!

"Jumping grasshoppers!" Johnny exclaimed. "If we could only help you!"

"I wish you could," said Jackson. "But I'm afraid you can't."

"Look," Johnny suggested, "why don't you come and search our house and the store building? Pop would let you. You might find something."

Jackson shook his head. "We did that, Johnny. We got permission from the owner before you came. We went over the whole place with a fine-toothed comb. There wasn't a thing."

He took his foot off the gas pedal and the jeep slowed to a stop. There were the two red gas pumps. Johnny sighed.

"Couldn't you stay just a little while?" he asked.

"Nope. Every minute counts. And, besides, I told you my father is against baseball, anyhow."

"Gee! Maybe if he saw us play, he'd understand how important it is," Johnny said.

Jackson laughed. "Not a chance. You kids will have to do the best you can by yourselves. Just remember this; practice every day and keep up your drills. Don't worry about playing games. That'll come later."

"But aren't you *ever* going to help us?"

"I'll try," said Jackson. "I'll come when I can. But I can't promise."

The boys climbed out. Jackson stepped on the gas. Then he was gone up the road.

Johnny and Buster silently walked across to the little stone house. Johnny took the key from under the step and unlocked the door. Then they stood still and stared at each other.

"Aw, shucks," said Johnny.

"That's what I think," said Buster.

"It's a darn shame," said Johnny. "Just when we get everything started—a club and a house and a coach,—this has to happen."

"Yes," said Buster. "Why couldn't Joe keep still? He's always bragging about something."

"Uh-huh," said Johnny. "He just can't keep his mouth shut." Then a new idea struck him. "No, that's not what I mean. It isn't a shame about Joe bragging. I don't mind that, if it makes the guys want to play better. It's a shame about Jackson's father making him read all those darn books."

Buster laughed. "That's funny. I was just thinking that would be interesting."

"You were!" Johnny exclaimed. "You must be crazy!"

"Could be," Buster admitted. "But I sure would like to know about this little old house. Maybe if Jackson goes and reads all those books in the Greenville Library, he'll find out."

Johnny sat down on a box, and sighed. "Yes, *maybe*. But I should think he'd find out more just sticking around here. Hey, I have an idea! Why don't we search the place?"

"That would be good," Buster agreed. "If we could find out something, then maybe Jackson's father would let him play with us."

"That's the ticket," said Johnny. "OK, you stay here and wait. I'll get some food for us and then we'll think of something."

Johnny ran to the house. "Hello, Mom," he said. "Buster and me, we're going to work in the club house this afternoon. Can we have some food? We're in a hurry. Oh, boy! Look at that cake!"

His mother cut two thick slices of cake and handed him two bottles of root beer.

Johnny ran back through the rain. He lit the

lamp, and the two boys sat on boxes and ate and drank. The rain beat on the roof. The wind whistled outside. The little lamp threw dancing shadows on the walls.

When they had finally licked the frosting and several layers of dirt off their fingers, they jumped up, ready for action.

"Well," Buster asked, "where do we look?"

And then, suddenly, they realized that they didn't know where to look and they didn't know what to look for.

Johnny's spirits sank. "I don't know," he answered. "Jackson said he and his father went over this place with a fine-toothed comb."

It was all right to talk about discovering something, but how were they going to do it? They'd just been talking big. After all, if Jackson and his father couldn't find anything, what could a couple of kids do?

"I guess we might as well forget it," he said, gloomily.

"Yes, I guess so," Buster agreed, looking at the floor.

"But what are we going to do now?" Johnny demanded. "We can't just sit here."

"We could read the rule books," said Buster.

"Aw, I don't feel like reading," said Johnny. "I want to *do* something."

"But what can we do?" Buster asked. "It's raining. I thought we'd read the rule books and I'd learn—"

Johnny interrupted. "I know. Let's clean up the joint. After all, it's our club house. And it's a mess." He waved his hand at the dust and dirt. "We'll sweep the floor and put up the pennants." He ran to a corner and seized a broom that was leaning there. "I'll sweep. Here's a rag. You can wipe off the counter. And look at all those spider webs in the windows. Clean 'em up."

He began to sweep up clouds of dust. The activity made him feel better. He swept faster.

Suddenly Buster sneezed. "*Kachoo!* Hey! Take it easy!"

But Johnny wouldn't. He kept right on. Soon he had a pile of dust and dried leaves and broken nut shells in the middle of the floor.

"Cut it out," Buster complained. "You're making such a draft you'll put the lamp out."

The lamp was flickering wildly, and the glass chimney was getting all smoked up.

Johnny stopped sweeping. But the lamp flame kept on flickering.

"It wasn't me," he said. "There's a wind from somewhere."

Buster looked all around. "How could there be a wind?" he asked. "The doors and windows are all shut."

"That's right," said Johnny. "Maybe it comes down the chimney." He walked over and held his hand in the fireplace. "I don't feel a thing," he said. "Besides, if there was a wind coming down the chimney, it would blow the ashes around."

Buster looked surprised at this. Sure enough, the ashes were lying still. But where was that breeze coming from? It seemed as if somebody were blowing on the lamp. And yet nothing was open.

The boys stared at each other. It was a little scary.

"Maybe it's coming through this other door," Buster suggested, pointing to the one behind the counter.

"That!" said Johnny. "Why, that's never been opened. There isn't a crack anywhere. Don't be dumb."

"Could we open it?" Buster asked.

"No," said Johnny. "Why should we? We'd just fall in the creek."

Buster looked thoughtful. "I'd like to know," he said, "why they made a door into the creek."

"Well," said Johnny, "you could just reach out the back door and get a bucket of water. Or you could stick a fishing pole out the door and catch a fish for supper. You could go fishing when it rained and not get wet."

Buster shook his head. That didn't make sense to him. "Suppose," he said, "there was a lot of rain in spring. That creek might get so full the water would come right in the back door. The whole house would get wet."

"You're right," said Johnny. "It doesn't make sense. It doesn't even make sense for the house to be built so close to the creek, even if there wasn't any back door. The water could leak in just the same."

"Well, there it is, anyhow," said Buster. "And there's another thing. Why does such a little house need two doors? The front door opens on the road and I should think that would be enough. You never use the back door."

"Well, I guess they must have used it when they

built the house," Johnny said.

Buster shook his head. He walked over and looked at the front door. Then he went back and examined the back door.

Then he said, "They're not the same."

"Of course, they're not the same," said Johnny. "One is the front door and the other is the back door."

"I know that, you dope," said Buster. "I mean they're different kinds of wood. Come over here and look."

Johnny remembered. He had noticed that before. The back door was made of rough hewn planks, fastened together with two cross bars that were merely split logs. They had been smoothed and planed down so that they had no bark left on them, and you wouldn't notice at first that they were logs, but they were. The front door was an ordinary pine door, with two thin panels and a brass door knob and lock. But the back door had a block of wood for a knob and a huge iron lock with a design of leaves and flowers molded into it.

"I never saw a lock like that," said Johnny. "It must be real old. I wonder—"

"What?" Buster asked.

"I wonder if Pop has the key. I never heard him talk about it."

"It would be a big key," said Buster. "Look at the size of that keyhole."

"Then I don't think he has," said Johnny. "I haven't seen any big key. Say, look! I bet—maybe—"

"Well, what?" Buster asked again.

"You were saying why should such a little house have two doors. Well, maybe when they built it, it only had *one* door. Because the front door is just like any house door but that back door is different."

"That's what *I* said," said Buster.

"And you said the front door opens on the road. Well, what if the road wasn't there when the house was built? Then they wouldn't need the front door. Maybe the back door was the front door."

Buster's face lit up. "That must be it!" he said. "Somebody put the front door in later, after the road was made. And they just left the old door there, all locked up. Gee! I guess we did figure something out, after all!"

"Yes," said Johnny, "but—but what of it?"

It was true, their discovery didn't seem to mean much, if it *was* a discovery. So the back door was older than the front door.

"And we still can't figure out why the old door was made opening right over the creek," said Buster. "If that was the only door, how would they get out? Maybe there was a bridge across the creek, leading right to the door."

"That's a crazy way to build a house," said Johnny. He was feeling tired from all this puzzling. "Come on," he said. "Let's finish cleaning up this mess."

He picked up the broom again and began to sweep the dirt into the fireplace. Then he bent down and looked at it.

"Look at all the nut shells," he said. "Somebody's been eating nuts."

"Must be squirrels in here," said Buster.

"Squirrels!" said Johnny. "How do you know?"

"They got into our attic," said Buster. "There were nut shells all over the floor. My mother was as mad as anything."

"But how could they get in here?" asked Johnny. "Everything is closed up tight except when we're here, and they don't come in then."

"Maybe they come in through the chimney," Buster suggested.

"Well, then, there would be nut shells in the fireplace," said Johnny, "and there aren't. Only over at the other end. There must be a hole someplace."

They stared up at the walls and down at the floor. There was not a crack large enough for a mouse.

Johnny leaned wearily back against the counter. "I give up," he said.

As he said it, something furry brushed the back of his head and landed behind him on the counter.

"Yow!" Johnny screeched and spun around.

There, with his tail swollen to twice its natural size, was Ted Williams!

Johnny's yell had scared him as much as he had scared Johnny.

Johnny stared wildly at Buster. "Where did he come from?" he demanded.

"From up there!" Buster cried, pointing to a spot over the back door.

"Then there must be a hole up there," said Johnny. "And I'm going to see where it is! Come on, help me."

Together they leaned against the counter and pushed it against the wall. Then they climbed up on it. Their heads touched the ceiling. Between the roof and the beam on which the rafters rested,

was a space. Johnny put his hand in.

"This is where the wind was coming from," he said. "But the wall must be broken on the outside, or how would Ted Williams get in?"

He pressed his head up to the ceiling and peered over the edge of the wall.

"There *is* a hole there," he said. "I can see daylight. Looks as if a stone is missing. But how come we never saw it from the outside?"

"The roof hangs down and hides it," said Buster.

"That's it," said Johnny. "Well, I guess that's how Ted Williams disappears so fast when Daniel

Boone chases him. That was pretty smart of him to find that hole. I guess he comes in here to keep out of the rain."

"And I guess that's where the squirrels come in," said Buster. "See if there are any nuts in there."

Johnny put his hand in the hole. Suddenly he gave another yell.

"What's the matter?" Buster asked.

"There's something in here," said Johnny. He pulled his hand out of the hole. In it were two things; a small black book and a big iron key.

8. A Triangular Stone

THE BOYS stood for a moment, staring at what Johnny held in his hand.

At last Johnny asked, "Where do you suppose they came from?"

"Somebody left them there," said Buster.

"Of course," said Johnny. "But who? The people who lived here before?"

Buster looked at the key. It was a big key, rusty, but there were still traces of a design on it—a design of flowers and leaves.

"I never saw a key like that," he said.

Johnny said, "Maybe the people who lived here

before came from some foreign country. Or maybe—"

A new idea came to him. He stared at Buster. He could see that Buster had the same idea.

"Maybe it belongs to that lock!" Buster exclaimed. He seized it and stuck it into the keyhole. It fitted! But it wouldn't turn.

"I guess the hole is rusty," said Johnny. "But it certainly looks as if they belonged together. Why was it put in that hole, though, and who put it there?"

"Why, whoever owned the house," said Buster. "He went out and put the key in that hole, just the way we put our key under the step when we go out. That's where he hid it."

"But the hole is over the door. How could he reach it?"

"Look how low that door is. A grown-up could reach it easily."

"You're right," Johnny said. "But it couldn't have been the man who sold the house to Pop, or he would have said something about it. It must have been a long time ago."

Buster nodded. "But if that hole has been there a long time," he said, "and squirrels have been going in and out, they would have knocked the key away."

"You're right again," said Johnny. "Gosh, you ought to be a detective."

"And, besides," Buster went on, "there would be a lot more nuts in here. So maybe the squirrels just started going in a little while ago."

"You mean," said Johnny, "that the hole was opened up just a little while ago?" He put the key and the book on the counter. "Come on. Let's go and see how it looks on the outside."

He ran out into the rain. Buster followed. They galloped over the footbridge to the other side of the brook and looked at the back of the house. There was nothing unusual to be seen. The big willow tree beside them leaned across the brook and dripped wetly on to the roof of the little house, and the overhanging eaves hid the part of the wall that was over the door.

"We'll have to get over there," said Johnny. "Come on, and don't slip."

They went back over the bridge and scrambled along the bank, keeping close to the stone wall of the house, until they reached the door. Then Johnny leaned back and looked up. Sure enough there was a hole—a sort of triangular hole in the stonework.

"Look at that," he said. "A stone is missing. You can see the rafters inside. The light of the lamp shines through."

"Let me get a look," said Buster. He tipped his head back to see for himself. The bank was slippery, and there wasn't much room to stand. So it wasn't surprising that Buster, bumping against Johnny, should cause him to lose his balance. Johnny, grabbing at Buster to steady himself, made Buster lose *his* balance, and suddenly down they went backwards into the brook.

The water was cold as ice. Johnny gasped with the shock and thrashed about, trying to get to his feet. At last he managed to get over on his hands and knees and stand up. Dripping and shivering, he looked around for Buster. Buster was dripping and shivering, too, but there was a grin on his face and in his hand he clutched a triangular stone!

Johnny forgot about the freezing water.

"Where'd you get that?" he shouted.

Buster laughed. "I grabbed the bottom of the brook and a piece came loose when I got up," he said.

"That's the missing stone," said Johnny. "I wonder how it got there. Fell out, I guess."

At that moment there were a shout and the sound of footsteps coming fast. It was Johnny's father.

"You boys get in the house!" he called. "What's the matter with you, anyhow? Don't you know it's too early to swim?"

He reached down and seized first Buster and then Johnny and dragged them out of the brook. Their teeth were chattering now and they ran dripping across the road and into the kitchen.

Mrs. Burton didn't waste any time. She took one look at them and threw some wood in the stove and began filling a tub with hot water.

"Charles," she ordered, "get blankets. And you two boys take your clothes off at once. The idea! Going swimming in April! And in the rain, too!"

"But Mom," Johnny began, "we weren't—"

"Don't argue with me," she said, rubbing him briskly with a rough towel, as Mr. Burton did the same for Buster.

"What are you holding on to that rock for?" Mr. Burton asked. "Give it to me, I'll throw it out."

But at this Johnny shouted, "No! Don't you throw it out! It's very important!"

"My goodness," said his mother. "What's so important about an old piece of rock? It's much more important that you shouldn't get pneumonia."

But she took the stone and put it on a shelf.

In a little while Johnny and Buster were warm and dry. Buster looked rather funny with Johnny's clothes hanging loosely on him. Mrs. Burton poured out cups of hot cocoa and made toasted cheese sandwiches on the stove, which she kept stoking with more wood. When it wouldn't get any hotter, she went for more sweaters.

Johnny protested. "Gosh, Mom, you want us to melt? It's as hot as a furnace in here."

"Well, you mustn't get a chill," she said.

"I guess you think this is Alaska and we fell in the Bering Sea," said Johnny. "Well, we didn't."

Buster said nothing. After all, he was a guest.

"Now," said Mrs. Burton, "tell us how you happened to fall into the brook."

Johnny began, "Well, Mom, you see, we wanted to—" And then he stopped. Suddenly it seemed as if he ought to tell Jackson first. This would be the way to help Jackson.

He looked up at his mother and father. "Would you mind," he asked, "if we didn't tell you right

now? It's got something to do with that book Jackson's father is writing. We want to tell him first. There's something we want to show him. Do you mind?"

His mother smiled and shook her head. "No, we don't mind, if you promise not to fall in the brook again or do anything foolish."

"Of course, we promise," said Johnny. "Now I have to call Jackson up. Come on, Buster."

He ran to the store, and Buster jumped up and followed. Mrs. Burton called after them, "Johnny! It's cold out there!" and ran after them with blankets.

She draped the blankets around them and said, "If you don't keep these on out here, you must come right back to the kitchen."

The boys stood at the phone like a couple of Indians, wrapped in their blankets. When the operator asked for the number, Johnny said, "Ugh!"

The operator said, "What?"

"Willow Creek 2175," said Johnny.

The phone rang a few times, and then a cross, loud voice said, "Hello! Yes? What is it?"

Johnny said timidly, "Is Jackson there?"

"Hello!" said the voice. "Speak up, please. What do you want?"

That must be Professor Sedgwick, Johnny thought. My, but he sounded cross! Hard of hearing, too.

Johnny shouted into the phone, "Can I speak to Jackson?"

"All right, all right," said the voice. "No need to shout. I'll call him. Andrew! The telephone! And if it's those boys, tell them you can *not* play baseball."

Johnny heard steps approaching and Jackson's voice saying, "Of course not, Father, it's raining." He seemed to be laughing. Then he came to the phone and said, "Hello."

Johnny said, "Jackson, this is Johnny. Listen. You have to come over right away."

"Well, I can't do that," said Jackson. "I'm very busy."

"Listen, Jackson, this is important. Buster and I found something."

"What is it?"

"Well, I can't tell you now," said Johnny. "You have to come and see."

Jackson's voice sounded as if he were trying hard to be patient. "Look, kid," he said. "This is no time for fooling. I'll see you tomorrow."

"I'm not fooling, honest," said Johnny. "But it's so exciting. Listen, Jackson, this may be a help to you. It's about our little stone house. We made a discovery."

Suddenly Jackson began to pay attention. "You did? You really mean it? Well, maybe I *can* get over there. All right. Wait for me." He hung up.

Ten minutes later the jeep stopped in front of the gas pumps and Jackson ran up the steps and down the hall to the kitchen. He said hello to Mr. and Mrs. Burton.

"I'm glad you could come," Mrs. Burton said.

"These boys think they've found something, but they won't tell us. They have to tell you first, and we're dying to know. So hurry up, Johnny."

"Yes," said Jackson, "and it had better be good. I had quite a time getting away. Father thought you wanted me to play baseball." He laughed. "Father certainly does hate baseball. He says it's the great American time-waster."

"Was he mad?" Johnny asked.

"Oh, no," said Jackson. "He never gets mad."

Johnny thought the professor certainly had sounded angry over the telephone, but he kept that to himself. "Come on," he said. "We'll show you." And he started for the door.

But his mother objected. "Oh, no! You're not going out again. I'm not going to have you getting sick."

"But Mom!" said Johnny. "It's terribly important. We can't show him here. We have to go back to the stone house."

"Yes, and fall in the brook again," she said.

Jackson came to the rescue. "I'll see that nothing happens to them," he promised. "We'll run out and come right back."

"Well, all right," Mrs. Burton consented. "But

they have to put on plenty of clothes." And she pulled another sweater over Johnny's head. Johnny wriggled but it did him no good. Buster in the meantime climbed up and got the stone off the shelf and then ran out, just in time to escape having another sweater put on him.

"What's that stone for?" Jackson asked. But the boys wouldn't tell.

"You'll find out," said Johnny. "Now, Buster, you keep Jackson out till I say you can come in." He ran ahead, climbed up on the counter and put the book and the key back into their hiding place. Then he shouted, "Come in!"

Buster opened the door and Jackson walked in, mystified.

"What's all this hocus-pocus?" he demanded. "What are you doing up there?"

Johnny put his hand into the hole and lifted out the key and the book.

"Look at these," he said, "and tell us if they aren't something good."

Johnny had expected Jackson to be surprised. But he hadn't thought he would be quite so thunderstruck. For a minute Jackson couldn't speak. He just stared.

At last he said, "Where did you get those?" in a hoarse voice.

"Right in that hole," Johnny said. "Ted Williams jumped down on me, and then we climbed up and found the hole."

"Great Caesar's ghost!" Jackson whispered.

"First we felt a draft," said Buster. "And we wondered where the squirrels came from. And then we wondered how come nobody ever found it before; so we went outside—"

"Come on, we'll show you," said Johnny, dragging Jackson outside and around to the back. "Only don't fall in the brook or Mom will make you put on all the clothes in the house. See up there!" He pointed to the hole.

"And here's the rock that fell out of there," said Buster.

"Great day in the morning!" said Jackson.

They went back inside.

"Kids," said Jackson, "it looks as if you discovered something, sure enough. It looks as if somebody left this house, and locked the door and put the key and the book in that hole, which he had made for a hiding place by loosening the stone. Then he

Johnny had expected Jackson to be surprised. But he hadn't thought he would be quite so thunderstruck

slipped the stone in, and there it has been ever since, until—"

"I know!" Johnny shouted. "Until Daniel Boone chased Ted Williams that first day you came here. Don't you remember, something went 'bang!' and then we couldn't find Ted Williams?"

"That's right," said Jackson. "And Daniel sat there, barking at the back of the house, wondering where that cat had gone!"

Johnny laughed. "I thought it was smart of Ted Williams to have found the hole. But he didn't find it. He made it."

Buster said, "What do you mean, he made it? I don't get you."

"You would if you'd been here," said Johnny. "Ted Williams was running away from the dog. He beat it over the bridge and around to the back of the house. He must have climbed up the tree and jumped down on the roof, and his claws caught hold of that loose stone and knocked it out. That was the crash we heard. Then when he found the hole was there, he went in."

Jackson picked up the key and turned it over in his hand.

"Is that key a hundred and fifty years old?" Buster

asked. "That's what you said the house was."

"I don't know," said Jackson. "It looks old. They certainly had locks and keys like that in the East around 1800. But out here in Ohio, the settlers had no locks. They fastened their doors with leather hinges and a wooden bar. Maybe a latchstring. But this—"

"Maybe the man who built this house brought his lock with him from the East," Buster said.

"Maybe," said Jackson, absently. He picked up the book and looked at it. "This is a Bible," he said.

"Oh," said Johnny. He wasn't particularly interested in that. It was a shabby-looking little book, much the worse for age and dampness. Carefully, so as not to break the binding, Jackson opened it in the middle. The pages were stained and mildewed. He turned them until he got to the title page.

"Look at that!" he said. "It was printed in England. No date, but it must be very old." Then he looked inside the cover. The boys peered over his shoulder. Some words were written here in faded ink, in a stiff, old-fashioned handwriting.

"What does that say?" Johnny asked.

Jackson bent his head close to the page. "All the esses look like effs," he said. "That makes it hard to read. Let's see. 'From his loving Mother, with prayers that God may ever bless and keep him, to my dear son, Henry Totten—' " He broke off and shouted, "Totten! *Totten!* Do you kids know what this means? This belonged to Totten! Yowee!"

Johnny had never seen a grown-up so excited. Jackson put the book on the counter and then jumped around like a Comanche Indian. He seized both boys and hugged them. Then he said, "I have to go call up Father right away! Wait till he sees this!"

Then Johnny thought of something. He hadn't told his own father yet, and, after all, it was his father's property.

"I—I think I'd better ask my Pop first," he stammered, feeling embarrassed.

Jackson understood at once. "I get it, kid," he said. "Come on. Your Pop must be wondering what we're doing out here so long, and your mother will be having a—er, I mean, she'll be worried."

They went back to the house and Jackson laid the key and the book on the kitchen table. Mr. and Mrs. Burton examined them.

"Well," said Mr. Burton, "suppose you tell us all about it."

"I'll be glad to," said Jackson. "These boys have made, I think, a very important discovery. The book my father is writing is about the history of Willow Creek, you know."

Mr. Burton nodded. "Johnny told us."

"And there's a Henry Totten mentioned in the records, but we haven't been able to find out anything about him. We thought if we could learn about him, it would explain some other things we don't understand. Now it looks as if this old Bible belonged to him."

He opened the book and pointed to the name written inside the cover.

"I see," said Mr. Burton. "I think you're right. It *is* important. And what do you want to do?"

"With your permission," said Jackson, "I'd like to show it to my father."

"I'd be glad to have you show it to him," said Mr. Burton. "I know your father. Very fine man. Interested in lots of things—"

"But not in baseball," Johnny broke in.

"That's true, I'm afraid," said Jackson. "He has no patience with sports. Thinks they ruin colleges. Can't understand why I like them. We argue about it now and then."

Suddenly Johnny jumped to his feet. "I got it! I got it!" he shouted.

"You got what?" his mother said. "I mean, you *have* what?"

"The idea," said Johnny. "Pop, you gotta, I mean you hafta do something for us. Look, Pop, don't you let Professor Sedgwick even *look* at this book till he signs an agreement—"

"Why, Johnny!" said his father. "You surprise me. Why, the Professor is a friend. I wouldn't think of—"

"Wait, let me finish. Look, Pop, we're in trouble. We need Jackson to coach us. Make his father agree that if he gets this stuff, Jackson is allowed to coach us an hour a day!"

Buster grinned. "Pretty smart, Johnny, old kid," he said.

Mr. Burton looked very doubtful, but Jackson said, "I think he's right. I think we owe these boys something for finding this stuff and realizing it was valuable. And we'll owe you something, too, if you let us use it."

"I wouldn't take anything for it," said Mr. Burton. "It's public property and belongs in a museum. But I *will* be glad if you can play ball with the boys once in a while. We like to have Johnny's friends out here."

"I like to come," said Jackson. "OK, boys, it's a deal."

9. 

A Message in Charcoal

"Now," said Mr. Burton, "let's have a look at what you've found, and then Jackson can take the book home to his father."

But Mrs. Burton stopped them. "Just a minute. It's five o'clock. Buster's mother will be wondering where he is. Suppose we call her up and ask if Buster may stay to supper. And Jackson, you stay, too."

Jackson began to protest. But Mrs. Burton opened the oven door. Inside was a meat pie that looked and smelled so good that he couldn't resist.

"All right," he said, "but I must go very soon after supper. I didn't tell Father how long I'd be away."

"We'll have an early supper," Mrs. Burton said. "Then we'll talk about the things and we won't have to stop for any interruptions. And Johnny," she called as the boys started for the telephone, "ask Buster's mother if he may stay overnight."

After the pie was gone, along with a good deal of milk and bread and butter and applesauce and doughnuts, the boys cleared the table and Jackson laid the little Bible and the key on it. They all drew their chairs nearer. Jackson opened the book and they looked again at the faded, slanting writing.

"There's no doubt that this belonged to Totten," he said. "In that case, the stone house may have belonged to Totten, too. Of course, it doesn't really *prove* it. Somebody else might have got hold of the Bible later and put it there. It would really make more sense if the stone house had been built later."

"Sure it would," said Buster. "A man couldn't build a stone house out in the woods. He'd have to go and find all the stones."

"Well, there are plenty of stones around here," Mr. Burton said. "I found that out, digging in the garden today. Why not use them?"

"But it takes too long to build a stone house," Buster said. "His family would be sitting around without a house, waiting for him to dig up the stones."

"Maybe he didn't have any family," Johnny suggested.

"Then what would he build such a fancy house for?" Mrs. Burton asked. "If he was just a man by himself, he'd build himself a lean-to rather than bother with a regular house."

"Maybe he was engaged," Mr. Burton said. "Perhaps he wanted some girl to marry him, and she said she would if he'd build her a better house than any of the neighbors had."

Mrs. Burton laughed. "You would think of that," she said. "But I understood there weren't any neighbors."

"Well, we don't know," said Jackson. "But let's see if we can find out anything from this Bible."

He turned the pages. Here and there a phrase was underlined.

"Looks as if Mr. Totten read his Bible," he said. "He liked the Psalms, apparently. Look at this: 'He turneth a wilderness into a pool of water, and a dry land into water-springs.' And here's another: 'The mountains skipped like rams, and the little hills like lambs.'"

"I remember that from Sunday school," said Mrs. Burton. "I used to sit and wonder how mountains could skip."

"What does it mean?" Johnny asked.

"Depends where he was when he underlined the words," his father said. "If he was here, it means he liked the country."

"Maybe there was a drought, and then it rained and the brook got full of water, like today," Johnny said.

"Yes," said Buster, "and then there was a nice day, you know, the kind that makes you want to jump around and you think even the ground wants to jump."

Jackson turned another page. "Look here," he said. " 'The stone which the builders rejected is become the head of the corner.' "

Mr. Burton said, "That could mean that the other people made fun of him for building a stone house."

" 'By the rivers of Babylon, there we sat down, yea we wept,' " Jackson read.

Johnny looked inquiringly at his mother.

"Maybe he was homesick," she guessed.

" 'Upon the willows we hanged up our harps,' "

said Jackson. "He's got that underlined twice. He must have liked willows."

"So he built his house near a willow," said Johnny.

"And by the waters of Babylon," said Jackson. "That means a strange land. But a minute ago we said he liked it here. So why should he weep?"

"That's an important question," said Mrs. Burton. "We have to find out why he should weep."

Johnny looked up at her to see if she was joking, but her face was quite serious. She really meant it.

Just then Jackson turned another page, and a thin sheet of paper fluttered to the floor. He picked it up. It was covered with writing. But it was the strangest kind of writing. Johnny had never seen anything like it. It wasn't just in lines like ordinary handwriting. It was all over.

"What kind of puzzle is that?" he asked.

"It isn't a puzzle," said Jackson. "It's an old letter."

"But why is it written like that?"

"Paper used to be scarce," said Jackson. "So after they had filled the page with writing, they turned it around and wrote across the page. Let's see if I can read it."

It was very hard to read. "Dear Henry," it began, "I pray that this letter finds you well as it leaves me, and that God will bless and keep you until we meet again. Our neighbor John Collins and his family are leaving in a wagon train for the Ohio country, so I take the opportunity of entrusting this letter to his care. John Collins plans to travel from Cumberland to Wheeling in Virginia, and then to take a boat to carry him down the river as far as Fort Washington."

"That's what they called Cincinnati," said Buster.

"That boy sure knows his history," said Jackson. "Maybe *you* had better help my father with his book. Well, let's go on. 'He will stop there, but will try to send this letter on further, though how anyone can expect to find your colony in the midst of the trackless woods, I cannot tell. I pray daily that you are safe from wild beasts and Indians.' "

"She was scared, wasn't she?" said Johnny.

"She had a right to be," said Mrs. Burton. "I can imagine how I'd feel if I were home in the East and Daddy were out here fighting Indians."

"How do you know the letter was from his wife?" Johnny asked. "It doesn't say so."

"Of course, it is," said his mother, indignantly.

"How could it be anybody else?"

"We'll see," said Jackson. " 'Timothy is much improved. His fever is gone, and though he is still weak, he grows stronger every day. We hope to go with the next wagon train to the westward. I shall be sorry to leave our pleasant stone house here in Maryland, with the willow tree by the door—' "

"Look at that!" Johnny cried. "A stone house with a willow tree!"

"Just like this one," his mother said, nodding.

" '—but glad, indeed, to see you again. This has been a cruel separation. God bless you, my dear husband. I am ever, and most affectionately, your loving wife, Martha Totten.' "

"What did I tell you?" Mrs. Burton exclaimed. "It's quite clear that she was his wife. She couldn't go with him because their son Timothy was sick. She wasn't too anxious to go anyhow, so William was building a stone house for her so that she should feel at home when she arrived. He was even lucky enough to find a willow tree for her. He was a very loving husband."

"But I should think she'd feel more at home closer to the neighbors," said Johnny. "Why did he build it out here?"

"Maybe he couldn't find any willows in town," said Jackson.

"Well, now we know why he might have felt like weeping," Mrs. Burton said. "He was wishing his family had been with him. Maybe he even thought he had made a mistake to come so far."

"I wonder if his family ever got here," Buster said.

"Well, let's see if there is any more information in here," said Jackson, carefully putting the letter back between the pages.

He turned some more pages. There were more phrases underlined. But there were no more letters. Jackson ruffled the pages to make sure. Then he turned over the last page. Inside the back cover, scrawled with a piece of charcoal, were the words, "Dig beneath the great willow on the west side nearest the stream—"

That was all.

The five of them sat there, staring at the words. What could they mean? Who had written them? Was it Henry Totten himself?

Whoever it was, he had been in a terrible hurry. He hadn't taken time to tell what to dig for. He hadn't finished the sentence. He hadn't even had time to find a pen but had scribbled in this treasured Bible with a piece of charred wood from the fireplace. And he had put the book with his key and gone away and never come back.

Why? That was the question.

Mr. Burton said, "It seems to me he must have been running away from something."

"Why, Pop?" Johnny asked.

"Because otherwise he would have dug it up himself, whatever it was, and taken it with him. But he had no time. What was he running from? A fire?"

"I don't think so," said Jackson. "There's no sign of fire having touched the house."

Suddenly Johnny remembered something. What was it the boys were always playing around here?

"Indians!" he exclaimed.

"I bet the kid is right," said Jackson. "Maybe there was an Indian raid. He must have buried something in the earth and run."

"But why did he leave a message in a book?" Mrs. Burton wondered.

"Don't you see? He might have expected to come back himself. But if he didn't get back, there must have been somebody else who knew where he always hid his key. And that person would go to get the

The five of them sat there, staring at the words. What could they mean? Who had written them?

key, and find the message in the book and dig up the treasure." Jackson jumped up from his chair. "Say, Mr. Burton, when can we start digging?"

"Right now," said Mr. Burton. "I can't wait another minute. I want to see what's there, as much as you do. Let's go out while there's still some light."

The boys jumped up, too.

"Now, boys," Mrs. Burton said, "you must put coats on—"

"OK, Buster," said Johnny, "here we go for the North Pole again."

They were just starting out when the phone rang. Mr. Burton answered it.

"It's for you, Jackson," he called. "I think it's your father."

They waited while Jackson went to the telephone. Through the receiver they could hear an angry voice. It went on for a while and then it stopped.

"No, I'm not playing baseball," Jackson answered. "I'm very busy. We've made a very important discovery. Listen, Father, stop shouting at me and get in the car and come down here. We're going to start digging for something. No. I won't tell you another word. I'll wait till you get here. Good-bye." He hung up.

"Will he come?" Johnny asked.

"You bet he will," said Jackson, grinning. "When I mentioned digging he started to get excited."

"Well, don't forget our agreement," Johnny reminded him.

Ten minutes later a car stopped in front of the house. Jackson went out to the porch to meet his father. The boys, waiting inside, heard a whispered conversation.

Then they heard some words. "Poppycock! Nonsense! I'm doing a serious work and you make arrangements with children!"

"This isn't nonsense," said Jackson. "It's valuable stuff and the boys deserve a reward."

"Oh, all right, all right," the Professor agreed. "But let me see what you've got."

Jackson brought his father inside and introduced him. From his voice, Johnny had expected to see a large, angry man. But the Professor was small and slender, with spectacles and white hair.

"Good evening, sir," he said to Johnny's father. "Sorry to put you to all this trouble."

"No trouble at all," said Mr. Burton. "Just take

a look at what these boys have found."

The Professor bent over the book. He opened it and looked at the writing inside the cover. He took out a magnifying glass. He wiped his forehead and whispered hoarsely. "Marvelous! Unbelievable! Priceless!"

But Jackson was in a hurry. "Look at this," he said, showing him the back cover.

Professor Sedgwick stared at it a moment and then said, "Well, what are we waiting for? Let's dig!"

They set out across the road. The rain had stopped. The sky was deep blue, and a rim of pink in the west showed where the sun had set. The birds were peeping in the dripping trees.

Mr. Burton got a pick and shovel to dig with. Mrs. Burton carried a large gasoline lantern. They walked across the footbridge.

"Now, let's see," said Mr. Burton, "the writing in the book said to dig on the west side of the willow. Is that right?"

"I thought it said on the side nearest the stream," said Jackson.

"But the willow is on the west side of the stream," said Johnny. "So the side nearest the stream is the east side."

"Maybe it means the west side of the house," said Mrs. Burton.

"But the west side of the house is right against the bank of the brook," Buster pointed out. "There isn't any room to dig."

"Well, there's only one thing to do," Jackson said, "and that's to start digging. I think we should start on the west side of the tree."

"But that's the side farthest from the stream," the Professor said. "There must be some mistake."

"It certainly doesn't sound right," Jackson said. But he plunged the pick into the earth. Mr. Burton shoveled the dirt away.

They dug and dug. Every time the pick hit something solid, the boys shouted, "There it is!" But each time it turned out to be a rock.

They dug a big hole on the west side of the tree.

Then they dug on the east side of the tree. It grew dark. The gasoline lantern shone like a spotlight on the turned-up piles of earth.

"My goodness, how deep is this thing buried, whatever it is?" Jackson demanded, pausing for a rest and wiping his moist face with a dirty hand. "The man was supposed to be in a hurry. How could he stop to dig all the way to China?"

At last they had a circle dug all around the tree. Mr. Burton straightened up and leaned on his spade. Jackson stood up and looked at him, and they shook their heads.

There was nothing there.

10.

The Secret at First Base

IT WAS hard to go to sleep. Johnny and Buster were so excited and there was so much to talk about that they simply weren't sleepy. Johnny couldn't remember a day when so much had happened. Beginning with the sweeping of the club-house floor and finishing with the excavation around the willow tree, there hadn't been a dull moment. Even the disappointment when they had failed to find anything had been like something out of a book. It simply meant that they had to look further.

The only question was, where? That was something nobody could answer. Professor Sedgwick had sat for a long time going over and over Henry Totten's Bible, trying to figure out something from the letter and the underlined words, but at last he had to admit defeat.

"I wonder if somebody put that there on purpose for a joke," Johnny whispered.

Buster shook his head in the dark. "I don't think so," he whispered back. "That Bible is good and old."

"But I mean the writing in the back," said Johnny.

"Well, maybe," said Buster. "But then we don't know what we were digging for. Maybe it's something that rotted away after all these years."

"A dead skunk, maybe?" Johnny suggested.

This seemed very funny and they had to stuff the bedclothes into their mouths to keep from laughing too loudly.

Then Buster said, "If it was, then the dirt that Jackson was smearing over his face was partly dead skunk."

That was so funny that loud laughs burst out.

Mrs. Burton's voice called downstairs, "You boys keep quiet and go to sleep."

After that they were careful to be more quiet. They were so quiet that it wasn't long before they were asleep.

When they woke up, sunshine was pouring in through the window.

They put on their clothes and ran out to look at the hole. There were the piles of dirt around the willow tree. The boys poked around with a stick, half hoping that in bright daylight they might turn up something that had been missed the night before. But there was nothing.

They ran off to look at the baseball field. It was still damp after all the rain. But the sun was shining so brightly that it seemed it must dry up in time for baseball practice that afternoon. Only the low place beyond the stump was *really* wet.

"But we can stay away from there," Johnny said. "Now we've got that agreement with Jackson, we can't afford to miss any practice."

"Let's not tell the fellows anything till they get here," said Buster. "I want to see the look on their faces when they find out."

"OK," Johnny agreed. "Only remember, no fooling around playing Indians. We have to play ball."

When the boys arrived in the afternoon, and saw the piles of dirt and the key and the book and heard the amazing story, the look on their faces was enough to satisfy anybody. Even Joe had nothing to say while Johnny and Buster told what had happened the day before.

And apparently they remembered that they had to take their ballplaying seriously, too. They cheered when they heard about the bargain Johnny had made with the Professor, and when Jackson said it was time to start they ran out to the middle of the field with no fooling at all.

But for once Daniel Boone was not with them. He was busy digging. He had discovered the holes around the willow tree, and now he was sniffing, shaking his head and digging busily with his front paws, shoveling the loose dirt out between his hind legs. He got dirt all over his nose, and sneezed and dug some more.

He's got the digging fever," Jackson said. "He gets it once in a while. He won't stop till he's worked it off. Just ignore him."

They started with batting practice. Howard, Charles and Max took their places in the field, while Johnny, Buster and Joe lined up at home plate.

"Now, kids," Jackson said, "forget that this is batting practice. Make believe it's a real game. I'm the opposing pitcher, and the enemy team is out there on the field, ready to put you out if they can.

Surely that hit was good for a home run

Give it everything you've got."

"OK, Coach," Johnny said. "Let's see what *you've* got."

Jackson pitched. Johnny swung with all his might. There was that satisfying smack, the ball sailed into the air and Johnny began to run. He approached first base. Nobody stopped him. He gave the old stump a slap with his hand and galloped on. Surely that hit was good for a home run. He rounded second. Still no ball. He steamed across home plate and stopped, panting for breath. Then he looked around. Everybody was searching for the ball.

"Come on and help us look," Buster called. "You hit it. You ought to be able to find it."

"What do you mean?" Johnny yelled. "You're supposed to keep your eyes open. I was busy running." But he ran across the field to help in the search.

They poked around in the grass, they stamped on the ground and beat around with the bat, but no ball.

The low place beyond the stump was still very wet.

"Maybe it floated away," Howard suggested.

"Don't be dumb," Johnny said. "How could it float?"

"Where's Daniel Boone?" Buster asked. "Maybe he could find it."

"That's a good idea," said Jackson. "Here, Daniel! Come on, boy. Get the ball."

Daniel came running, wagging his tail.

"Find the ball," Jackson said, pointing to the ground out beyond the stump.

Daniel wagged his tail harder. He wagged his whole body. But he didn't move. He just stood and looked at Jackson.

Jackson laughed. "He doesn't know what I want," he explained. "He knows I want him to do something but he doesn't understand what. Get the ball, Daniel," he ordered again, pointing to the ground.

Suddenly Daniel got an idea. He put his nose to the ground and trotted around, sniffing. About halfway between the stump and the low place he began to dig.

"No, no, I didn't tell you to dig!" Jackson said.

But Daniel paid no attention. He went on digging.

"I guess once he starts digging," Buster said, "that's all he wants to do."

"Look what a big hole he's made already," said Joe.

"Isn't that the place he was digging in last week?" Howard asked. "Remember, you made him stop, Jackson."

Jackson nodded. They gathered around Daniel and watched him work. He went at it like a little steam shovel.

"But I don't see," said Johnny, "how he could make such a big hole in just a couple of minutes." He bent over. "Say!" he said. "There was a hole there to begin with. That's why it's so deep. How come we never saw it?"

"It was hidden by the grass," said Charles.

Daniel stopped digging. He stuck his nose in the hole and pulled something out. Then he wagged his tail and laid the thing down at Jackson's feet.

"It's the ball!" the boys yelled. "He found it!"

"Good dog!" said Jackson, patting him. "You'll get a bone when we get home."

The boys squatted down and tried to make a fuss over Daniel, but he paid no attention. He turned back to the hole and began to dig again. In a few minutes he pulled something else out. It looked like a lump of mud.

"It's the first ball!" said Johnny. "They both fell in the same hole!"

"But how could they?" Buster asked.

"The ground slopes," said Jackson. "It slopes right down in the direction of the hole, so a ball would naturally roll that way and roll right into the hole."

"What is it, a woodchuck hole?" Howard asked.

"Looks more like a rabbit hole," said Jackson, slowly. He turned and stared at the stump, and then he walked around and then he came and felt the side of the stump. He seemed to have an idea.

"What's the matter?" Johnny asked.

"This stump," said Jackson. "It's a willow stump."

"It is?" said Johnny. "How can you tell?"

"By the bark," said Jackson.

"That's right," said Howard. "You can always tell a tree by the bark."

"I think," said Max, "is easier to tell a dog by the bark."

"No, *silly,*" said Howard, "we're talking about the stuff on the outside of a tree. Here. See this? Well, it's just the same as that big tree over by the stone house. You can tell that's a willow by the leaves, but this has no leaves so you tell by the bark."

"Oh!" said Max, solemnly. "Now is clear to me. I am much obliged." He made a bow.

"He's kidding you," Charles explained to his brother.

But Jackson had no time for jokes. "Look here, you two naturalists," he said. "Do you know how to tell the age of a tree?"

"Sure," said Charles. "Cut it down and count the rings."

"Well, how old would you say this stump was when it was cut?"

The boys gathered around the stump and began

to count. It was a slow job. Sometimes it was hard to see where one ring left off and the next began. When they got to fifty, Jackson stopped them.

"Look," he said. "You've counted about a quarter. That means this tree was about two hundred years old when it was cut down."

"Whew!" Johnny whistled. "How old is the one by the house?"

"You can see for yourself that it's smaller around than this stump," said Jackson. "It's about a hundred and fifty years old."

"But then," said Buster, "a hundred and fifty years ago it wasn't any more than a twig."

"That's right," Jackson said. "It may have been a sapling a few years old. Maybe it's a hundred and fifty-five now."

"But then," said Johnny, "when that man wrote in the book that we should dig near the great willow, he couldn't have meant the one by the house."

"But he must have," Buster exclaimed. "It says 'the great willow by the brook', and the brook is over there!"

Johnny suddenly saw what Jackson was driving at. "But don't you see," he cried, "it says 'dig on the west side of the willow nearest the brook.' So it *couldn't* be that one by the house."

"But it has to be near the brook," Buster insisted.

"What I think," said Jackson, "is that the brook moved."

"The brook!" the boys squeaked in chorus. "How could you move a brook?"

"Something might happen to change the course of a stream," said Jackson. "Look at that low place where it's so wet. What does it look like?"

The boys turned and looked. With all that water in it, it certainly looked like an old brook bed.

"Come on," said Jackson. "We're going on a little exploring trip. We're going to follow the brook and see where it goes to."

They walked across the field to the brook and then started upstream. The brook ran in a ditch beside the road for a way. Then it wandered off across a field. The ground rose sharply, and the boys climbed the hill, puffing to keep pace with Jackson's long stride.

The water splashed noisily down the hill. A couple of cows, peacefully eating grass, looked up in surprise to see a crowd of boys rush by.

They climbed higher and higher. It was a rocky pasture, with big and little boulders here and there among the blackberry vines.

At the top of the hill was a grove of trees. And just in the shadow of the trees was the biggest boulder of all. Jackson hurried up the hill to the boulder. A huge log lay over the top of it, and from somewhere underneath the water bubbled out.

The boys looked all around.

"Where's the brook now?" Johnny asked. "I can't see it anywhere."

Whenever it came to something connected with brooks or frogs or trees, the twins knew the answer.

"This is where it starts," Howard said. "It's a spring."

"It comes right out from under that big rock," said Charles.

"You're right," said Jackson. "And now let's see what kind of detectives you are. Can you tell what happened?"

Johnny didn't know quite so much about nature but he had seen lots of movies. He was a better detective.

"The tree fell down on the rock," he said. "It pushed the rock over on top of the spring, and that's why the water comes from underneath."

"It changed the course of the brook," said Jackson. "I'm not sure what made the tree fall—"

"Struck by lightning," said Howard.

"You're quite right," said Jackson.

"Well, why did the brook have to flow right back of the house that way?" Buster asked. "It might have its course changed, but why did it go just there?"

"I know," Charles said. "It ran into the lowest place it could find, and that was the ditch."

"So now," said Johnny, "the writing in the book means we should dig west of the old stump, and that place where it's all wet must be where the stream used to be, so it's between the stump and the wet place."

"You sum it up correctly," said Jackson.

"Then what are we waiting for?" Johnny shouted. And he started running down the hill, with the others at his heels.

The two cows stared at them as they rushed by. Down through the fields they galloped. Johnny ran for a shovel, and Jackson began to dig.

"Might as well go on where Daniel started," he said, piling up the dirt as fast as he could.

Suddenly the shovel went down into empty space and the earth caved into the hole.

"That must have been a rabbit hole there," said Jackson. "That's why Daniel was so interested."

"And the two balls just rolled in," said Johnny. "Are you going to dig any more?"

"Yes," said Jackson. "I'll go on and get this loose dirt out of here. But there's no use digging down *too* far. We mustn't forget that Mr. Totten left in a hurry. At least that's the theory we're working on—"

As he spoke, the shovel clanked on something.

"Go on, it's only a rock," said Johnny, remembering the day before.

But it was not a rock. Jackson laid down the shovel. He bent and lifted out of the earth, an old iron box.

11.

The Old Iron Box

THE BOYS watched in silence as Jackson brushed the dirt from the top of the box. They could hardly believe it. To think that this box had lain in the earth, under their baseball field, all this time and that nobody had known of it except perhaps the rabbits!

And Daniel Boone. Daniel stood by, wagging his tail, waiting to see what would happen next. They all waited for Jackson to speak. But he stood there like a man in a dream.

Finally Johnny couldn't stand it any more.

"Aren't you going to open it?" he asked.

Jackson seemed to wake from his dream. He looked up at the boys and then said, "Oh, yes! Of course. We must go to the house. We've got to show it to your parents and call up my father and tell him to come down."

He started across the field.

Twenty minutes later, Professor Sedgwick's car screeched to a stop. The Professor hurried in. He looked at the group gathered in the kitchen. Then he looked at the dirty old box that stood on the newspaper-covered table.

"Where did you find that?" he demanded.

"In the baseball field, Father," Jackson answered. "Right at first base!"

"Well," said the Professor, "it appears that baseball is some use, after all."

Jackson laughed. "I'm glad you're convinced, Father," he said. "But wait till we open it. If there's nothing good inside, then you won't think so much of baseball, after all."

"Well, open it," said his father. "What are you waiting for?"

The box was fastened with a rusty old hasp through which a nail had been slid. It wouldn't come out. Mr. Burton pushed a screwdriver under it and it broke open. He tried to lift the lid off, but it was stuck fast with rust. He pried it with his screwdriver, and suddenly the rusty old hinges burst apart. Boys and grown-ups leaned forward eagerly to look inside.

There was a bundle wrapped in some moldy cloth. And there were two ancient leather bags that crumbled to dust when Jackson tried to lift them.

Carefully, with both hands cupped underneath, he lifted out one of the bags and laid it on the newspaper. Between the bits of moldy leather, corn kernels poured out, ancient and hard as little stones.

"What's that for?" Johnny asked.

"Seed corn," said the Professor. "That must have been one of their most valuable treasures. If they lost that, they had no chance of a crop. No bread for a year."

Mr. Burton said, "It doesn't look a bit like that stuff you sold me a few weeks ago."

"No, it doesn't," said the Professor. "Much smaller. Look at this." He stuck his hand into the bag and pulled out what looked like two sticks of wood, about four inches long. "Corn cobs!" he said.

"Those little things?" the boys exclaimed.

"Yes, sir," said the Professor. "This is what corn used to look like. It wasn't always the great big stuff we have now."

Then he put his hand into the other bag and

pulled out a fistful of flat, irregular objects.

"Marvelous!" he gasped. "Priceless!"

"But what are those things?" Johnny asked. They looked like a lot of old junk metal—tarnished, black and moldy.

"Money!" said the Professor. "Antique coins."

"But look at the funny shapes!"

"Look at this one, like a half-moon!"

"That's the way they used to make change," the Professor said. "By chopping the coins in half. And sometimes people would shave off pieces of coins and melt down the shavings and sell them. That's how they got so irregular. This is worth a fortune!"

The boys' eyes were round with amazement. A lot of old corn was interesting, but this was real treasure. It was better than a movie.

"How can you tell?" Mr. Burton asked. "Are you sure they're genuine?"

"Look here," said the Professor. He took out a knife and scraped at one of the coins. The bright color of gold shone through the black tarnish. He looked at it through a magnifying glass. "It's a Spanish pistole," he said.

"Spanish!" said Joe. "Weren't they Americans? Why did they have Spanish money?"

"There wasn't any regular American money then," the Professor explained. "They used any kind they could get. I guess this thing was worth about four dollars. Now it's worth a lot more."

"Do you mean it?" said Mr. Burton.

"I certainly do. Here are some more. And look at this! It's a doubloon!"

"Like pirates had," said Buster. "Do you suppose Henry Totten was a pirate?"

The Professor laughed. "Of course not. But pirates liked to get hold of them when they could. Look at this one. It's a silver shilling. And here are some English sixpences. Of course, those aren't so valuable."

"Now we know why the townspeople were so anxious to find Henry Totten," said Mr. Burton. "They thought he'd run off with their money."

"Maybe it was his," said Mrs. Burton.

"I shouldn't think one man would have all this," said the Professor. "I think he must have been something like the Treasurer for the whole colony. Let's see now, what's this other thing?"

He lifted out the bundle and felt it. His face broke into a joyful smile. Johnny watched him. He had been excited enough over the money. This must be just as good. What could it be?

The Professor's fingers actually trembled with excitement as he loosened the folds of the cloth and drew out—a book!

The boys looked at each other in disappointment. Just a book? Was that anything important compared with a hoard of buried treasure? Apparently the grown-ups thought so. They were waiting breathlessly for the Professor to open the book.

The Professor turned back the cover. It was not a printed book. It was a copy book, with ruled pages, covered with faded writing in a careful, slanted hand. He pointed to the first line and read: " 'The record of the settlement on the banks of Willow Creek. Kept by me, Henry Totten, in accordance with the decision of the settlers.' "

The Professor sank back into his chair. For a moment he was speechless. Then he turned to his son.

"Andrew," he said, "this is what we've been looking for. This—this—it's wonderful! It's—" He couldn't finish.

He bent his head to examine the book again. The others sat quietly around the table, waiting. Then he began to read.

" 'August 1, 1795. Our river journey is ended. This day we unloaded our wagons from the barges on which we have floated down the river from Wheeling. We purchased supplies in Fort Washington. A flourishing town. Commenced our land travels once more. Bound for our tract, not far distant from Fort Greenville. All six families well and happy to be on land again.

" 'August 10. Traveling has become very hard. The road is little more than a trace. Most prefer to walk, as the jolting of the wagons makes riding too hard. We chop out trees as we go.

" 'August 16. Stopped at a settlement called Spring Hill.' "

"Spring Hill!" Buster interrupted. "Was that there then?"

"Apparently it was," said the Professor. "That gives me another idea. Maybe I can get some information over there."

"But we've seen the Spring Hill records, Father," Jackson said.

"I know," his father answered, "but now, in the light of this, we may understand them better. Well, let's go on.

" '—A settlement called Spring Hill. Many hospitable people there. The women took the opportunity to do their washing. The people are happy to have visitors, and several of the men offer to go with us to our own tract, which is but five miles distant. I can hardly believe that we are so near.

" 'August 17. This day we arrived at our destination, and gave thanks to the Almighty for our safe journey. If only my dear wife and son were with me, I should be happy. Again I wonder whether I have done right to leave them to come alone. But it seems I could do nothing else. Having promised to lead the party, I could not break my word.' "

"Now we know why he came without them," said Mrs. Burton. The Professor nodded and went on.

" 'I shall have our home built by the time they arrive. It is a beautiful spot. A cleared field with a brook running through it, and a good sized willow tree in the center. Many willows along the brook. Martha will be happy when she sees them.

" 'August 20. All the men in our party are busy cutting trees. We shall soon raise the first cabin. We must have all the cabins ready before cold weather. I shall live with the Loomis family. I have been asked to keep the money of all of our party. I am happy to see that my friends trust me. They must be very sure I shall not abscond.' "

"Abscond!" Buster broke in. "What's that?"

"It means to run away," said the Professor. "Apparently that's what they did think later."

"Well, go on," Johnny said. "This is like a serial story. I want to know what happened."

The Professor read on.

" 'August 25. A hunter passed by yesterday. Seemed surprised to see our settlement. He had been south to Fort Washington for supplies, and was bound north for the winter hunting. He had not been this way for a year. Asked about Indians. I told him we had seen none. He was astonished that we had not. Said that this place used to be one of their villages. This explains its level, cleared appearance. The hunter thought the Indians would return. However, since General Wayne's victory over them last year, we surely are safe.

" 'August 26. We have decided to build our cabins more or less in a circle on the edges of our cleared field. In the spring we shall use the field as a garden for the entire settlement and clear more land as fast as it can be done. Of course, we have arrived too late for planting now. There were so many delays in setting out. But we shall have enough grain to last the winter, and with God's help we shall have plenty of meat. We must gather hay for the beasts.

" 'September 5. The women have been gathering acorns and nuts. There are also wild berries and wild plums, as well as grapes in the woods. There are many nut trees, and we have even found some papaws and persimmons. These will help us through the winter. Our store of seed corn is safe in my strong box, with the money that has been put into my keeping.' "

"Just the way we found them," said Mr. Burton. "Do you suppose they never got around to planting?"

"We shall see," said the Professor.

He read on. Now and then he stopped where the writing had faded or a stain had blotted out some words. Then he went on. It was a story of courage and hard work.

There were storms. A cow was lost in the woods. There were fever and ague, and the mosquitoes were very thick.

Somebody was hit by a falling tree but, by good luck, escaped with only a broken arm, which Totten set for him.

John Loomis's cow had a calf. Totten had to help with that.

The wife of Thomas Carmichael had a baby. Totten christened it.

A post rider went by, and all in the settlement sent letters home. Totten thought the letters would arrive in about six months' time.

A circuit preacher came one day and held prayer meeting. Everybody was glad of that. It was such a long time since they had been able to go to church.

Then there was an entry about the end of October.

" 'I have decided to build a stone house. There are many stones hereabouts, piled up in heaps. No doubt the Indians who cleared this field left them there. And on a nearby hill are many more. Since I have been living in John Loomis's cabin, I have had no need to build my own, and now in the winter I shall have time for the work. Martha will feel more at home in a stone house, and I will plant a willow tree by the door so that she can sometimes think she is back in Maryland.' "

"What did I tell you?" Mrs. Burton asked, smiling.

"You were right, Mom," said Johnny. "I guess he

figured he would have nothing to do all winter so he might as well build a stone house—"

"Nothing to do!" his father exclaimed. "Why, he was the busiest man in the whole place. Go on, Professor."

The Professor read on.

" 'Henry Morrison will build the chimney as he has built all the others—' "

"Henry Morrison!" Jackson cried. "Why, he's one of the Willow Creek men! We have his initials on some of the chimneys in town!"

"But you know what this means!" the Professor said. "It means that everything we've thought about Willow Creek happened in reverse. We thought this stone house was built by somebody who came out from town. But it wasn't. The original settlement was right here. Henry Morrison was one of the original settlers. And for some reason they left this place and built again where the town is now."

"And the stone house wasn't all alone. There were a lot of log cabins besides!" Jackson said.

"But what happened to all the log cabins?" Johnny asked.

"Burnt down," Buster guessed.

"Maybe a hurricane came and knocked them all down," said Joe.

"Go on!" exclaimed Charles. "How could a hurricane knock down a bunch of log cabins?"

"We'll let the Professor continue," said Mr. Burton. "Maybe we'll find out."

The Professor went on.

" 'November 20. My house is growing fast. All my good friends are helping. Even the children bring stones. Young Johnny Loomis promises to shoot a bear so that his friend Timothy can have the skin for a bed cover when he arrives in the spring. If only I could hear that he is well and that Martha really is not afraid to make the long trip here, I should have nothing more to wish for.' "

"I guess that was on the poor man's mind all the time," Mrs. Burton said. "I wonder why he didn't plan to go home and get them."

"I guess he was afraid the rest of them couldn't get along without him," said Mr. Burton.

The Professor read on. The winter passed. There were blizzards and bitter cold weather. Wolves and bears were seen. An old man died. Two more babies were born.

Henry Totten's house was finished. In February

there was an entry.

" 'I have made a door for my house, and put on the lock which was once on my grandfather's house in Pennsylvania. Loomis laughs at me and asks whether I think thieves are coming to steal my wealth, here in the woods. I have made a hiding hole for the key above the door, such as we had at our former home. When Martha arrives, I will let her find the key and unlock the door herself. She will know where to look for it.' "

Johnny couldn't hold in his excitement. "Golly!" he cried. "It all fits in like the pieces of a puzzle. But then if she knew where to look, why didn't she—"

"Wait a minute," said Jackson. "Hold your horses. Go on, Father."

" 'March 1,' " the Professor read. " 'A spring-like day. Birds are beginning to come. No buds on the trees yet, but soon we shall begin to prepare for the spring planting. The ice on the brook is breaking.

" 'March 2. Loomis and I had good hunting today. Brought in a dozen rabbits. The ground is almost soft enough for the plough. I have dug up a willow sapling and planted it by the door.

" 'March 3. Johnny Loomis and George Carmichael, playing in the woods, told of seeing the remains of a campfire. No strangers have been near. Doubtless a hunter on his way to Fort Washington. But it is odd that he did not visit us.

" 'March 20. A post rider came through today. He brought me a letter from Martha. What a wonderful thing this is! Here in the midst of the wilderness I have received a letter written by her own hand! It took only three months to get here. Perhaps in three months more I shall see her.

" 'April 1. This day we broke ground. Ploughed half our field. Still too early to plant, but when the weather is a little warmer we shall be ready. The earth is black and rich. We have done well to choose this site, though there is some ague about, owing to the low situation of the land and the stream.

" 'April 3. Next week we are bidden to a wedding at the Spring Hill settlement. There will be a house raising for the newly wedded pair. We can ill spare the time, but it is long since we have had a holiday and we cannot refuse our neighbors.

" 'April 4. An Indian appeared today. He begged for food and tobacco, which we gave him, and asked for a gun, and some rum, which we did not. He was a poor object, ragged and dirty, and so ill fed that

"'This is the first Indian we have seen since we came'"

every rib in his body could be seen. This is the first Indian we have seen since we came. Our General Wayne has surely frightened them off. We asked the man where his people were, but he either could not or would not answer.

" 'April 9. Loomis and I have determined to remain here while the others go to the house-raising. If any Indians are about, we shall frighten them off.' "

The Professor stopped reading. Everybody waited.

"Well," urged Jackson, "go on. Don't stop now!'

"I can't help it," said his father.

"What's the matter?"

"There isn't any more!"

"Isn't any more?"

"No." The Professor pointed to the book. The writing had ended. The rest of the page was blank.

Everybody sat still.

Finally Jackson said, "Look through the rest of the book, Father. Maybe he goes on somewhere else."

The Professor turned every page. They looked in the box again. They looked into the bags. There was nothing.

The Professor drew a long sigh. "I think," he said, "that that's all we'll find out for sure. We'll have to guess the rest. And I don't think it will be too hard to guess."

"You mean," Johnny said, "that something happened?"

"Indians!" exclaimed Buster.

"That's what it looks like," said the Professor. "That lone Indian coming to beg. He must have been a spy. That field used to belong to them, the hunter said so. And they wanted it back. So they sent a spy to see how many people there were—"

"And when the people all went off to the wedding," said Johnny, "and Loomis and Henry Totten were there alone, the Indians came—"

"But General Wayne conquered the Indians!" Joe objected. "They made a treaty. They promised to go away."

"Yes, the chiefs promised," said the Professor. "But there were still plenty of Indian raids here and there. Little ones. Just a few poor Indians trying to keep from starving to death. They thought they had a right to get what they could from the settlers. Just the way the settlers thought they had a right to shoot any Indian they saw."

"But that isn't right!" said Johnny.

"It was a war," said the Professor sadly. "No war is ever right. Each side thinks the other is out to kill him and thinks he's got to kill his enemy first to keep from being killed himself, and they get to hate each other worse and worse and get more and more afraid. The white men won because they were stronger and smarter. Well!" He shook his head. "That's all over now. We've got to figure out what happened."

"Well," said Jackson, "this is what I think happened. Here are two men alone, and the Indians come. The two men hide in the stone house. That's safest. The Indians set fire to the cabins. The two men shoot till their bullets give out. After they stop shooting, the Indians think they are dead. Of course, the Indians might have set fire to the roof of the stone house. Or maybe they were so impressed with the stone house that they let it alone. Somehow Loomis got away, but Totten stayed to hold the fort. Now it seems to me that the rest of the people didn't come back."

"How did you figure out all that?" Mr. Burton asked.

"This is how," said Jackson. "In the earliest records that we have in town, somebody writes: 'Loomis made a secret visit to Totten's house.' How could he have done that unless he first escaped to warn the people about the raid? Totten must have stayed. Maybe he was wounded and couldn't get away. Loomis escaped and told them, and they were afraid to go back. There were only six families. They couldn't fight a tribe of Indians. So they started building over again where the town of Willow Creek is now. And then Loomis tried to steal back to see if he could find out what had become of Totten. The Indians must still have been there."

"What do you think the people did when they heard?" Joe asked. "Why didn't they all go and fight the Indians?"

"They weren't soldiers," said Jackson. "Maybe they sent somebody to get the soldiers from Fort Greenville. But maybe the soldiers were off somewhere, fighting Indians in another place. Maybe the Indians knew that, and that's why they came just then."

"So then what happened, do you think?" Howard asked.

"Well, I'm only guessing, of course," said Jackson. "But perhaps the people stayed a while at Spring Hill. And then they started a new settlement. I suppose the Spring Hill people gave them the things they needed, like seeds and tools. There's an entry that says Morrison went to Spring Hill for corn. Those Indians must have destroyed every single thing."

"And I bet," said Buster, "the Indians were just waiting for the people to come back. That's why Loomis had to warn them to stay away."

"That's right," said Charles, excitedly. "And Totten had to stay there to cover up Loomis's escape. Just like in the movies. The enemy sees the man in the house. They keep firing at him and they don't see the other guy escape."

"And then," said Howard, "when it gets dark and the Indians fall asleep, Totten tries to get away."

"That's right," said Johnny. "He puts the valuable things in the box, and he goes out and locks the door so the Indians will think he's still in there, and he hides the key in the hole over the door and puts the stone back. Then he buries the box, because it's too heavy to carry in the woods, and then he thinks of leaving a message and he runs back and grabs a piece of charcoal from a fire—"

"What fire?" Joe asked.

"Maybe one of the Indians' fires," said Howard, "because they're all asleep."

"Sure," said Johnny. "And the only thing he has to write on is the Bible, and before he gets finished the Indians wake up and he chucks the Bible in the hole with the key and runs."

"I guess he hoped somebody would find it," Buster said. "I bet he was sorry he'd never showed anyone where the hole was."

"There's one thing I don't understand," Mrs. Burton said, "and that is, how did he have time to dig a hole by the stump and bury that box, with the Indians all around? The ground must have been hard, and he would have made a noise—"

"No, Mom," said Johnny, "the ground wasn't hard! They'd just plowed it up. All he had to do was scoop the earth out with his hands. If he'd had to dig a new hole, the Indians would have seen where it was in the morning and taken the stuff away. But it was just a lot of loose earth, so it didn't look any different."

"The boy's right," said Mr. Burton, patting his son proudly on the back. "Smart fellow! Takes after me."

"Is that so!" said Mrs. Burton, indignantly. "Who figured out about Mrs. Totten, I'd like to know?"

"Oh, all right, have it your way," Mr. Burton said, smiling. "If you're so clever, what happened to Totten?"

"That we'll never know," said the Professor, "and we can't even figure it out. Maybe he was caught. Maybe the Indians took him prisoner and made him live with them. Or maybe he was wounded and died. Or maybe he got back home to Maryland somehow."

"I don't think so," said Johnny. "He would have found his friends first and told them where the money was."

"What about his wife?" Mrs. Burton asked.

"I guess she never arrived," said the Professor. "If she had, she would have found the key. She was the only one who knew where to look. So the house just stayed locked up."

"And then," said Johnny, "after about a hundred years the brook changed its course, and some people came to live here, and they made the road where it is now and made another door."

"And then they built the farmhouse," his father continued, "and used the stone house for a store, and then we moved out here; and that's the end of the story."

It was getting dark. Mrs. Burton got up and lit the lamp.

The Professor rose, too. "It's time to go," he said. "May I take these things with me?"

"Why ask me, Professor?" Mr. Burton answered. "Of course you may."

"They're your property," said the Professor. "They were found on your land. Of course, if you want to give them to the state for a museum, I'm sure you'll get quite a lot for them. They're really valuable."

"Well, if I do get something," said Mr. Burton, "the boys should have part of it. They made the discovery."

Suddenly Johnny's eyes flashed. "Oh, Pop!" he said.

Mr. Burton laughed. "Look how happy he is at the idea of getting some money."

"That wasn't it, at all," said Johnny indignantly. "I just had an idea."

"Well, what was it?" Jackson asked.

"I was thinking," said Johnny, "why couldn't we write to somebody in Maryland and find out if they know anything about Mr. Totten's family?"

The Professor sat down again and grinned at Johnny. "Young man, you have the right idea. Of course we can. Let's see. Cumberland, they came from. Totten. That's not such a common name. Sounds Dutch. And his grandfather was from Pennsylvania. Maybe his son stayed in Cumberland, and raised a family and—"

"Come on, Father," said Jackson, taking the Professor's arm. "Don't get started on that chapter today. We've got to take these boys home."

"That's right, that's right," said the Professor. "But we'll do it. Never fear. If there's anything to be learned, we'll find out."

He started for the door. Suddenly he turned back "There's just one thing I want to say before I go," he announced.

Everybody waited to hear what it was.

"I want to take back everything I ever said about baseball."

12.

Back to Baseball

It was Thursday afternoon and the bell had just rung. Johnny stood up and put his papers away in his desk and packed up his books. He felt good. They had just had a history test, and Johnny had answered every question. He didn't seem to mind history so much now. It made it different when history happened right in your own back yard.

And certainly there had been enough happening all week. People from the college had come out and examined the stone house and the brook and the stump. Reporters had come out to write stories, and photographers, to take pictures. They had bought lots of soda at Mr. Burton's store and told the boys how smart they were. The treasure had been put on exhibit in the town hall, and everybody had come to see it, and the Willow Creek Braves had been the center of attention. Everybody had talked to them, even the big boys.

Johnny was beginning to think that the big boys weren't a bad lot, after all. You could even get to like them. But it would not do for the Braves to forget that they had a game to play with them. And the Braves were very much out of practice.

Johnny hurried. Jackson would be waiting, and they were going to have a good afternoon of practice. From now on they mustn't waste any more time. He ran out and waited on the steps for the others.

"Come on, guys," he urged as they appeared. "No time to waste."

They didn't answer. They just stood there.

"What's the matter?" Johnny asked.

All five boys stood looking at him glumly. Johnny was getting more and more puzzled and alarmed.

"Well, come on," he said. "What's wrong? Let's get going. We have to play ball today."

"That's the trouble," said Buster. "Playing ball."

"What's wrong with that?" Johnny asked. "The Oak Street boys—"

Joe shuffled his feet. "Yes, them," he said, dejectedly. "My brother just told me they don't wanna play with us because we have only six men."

"Well, it's not so good," Johnny admitted. "But what can we do? If *we're* willing, I don't see why they should care. And if we can have Jackson pitch for us—"

"They say they don't want to waste time on a baby game," Joe said. "Either they play with nine men or not at all, and they can't play with nine men unless we have nine. It's all my fault. Why didn't I keep my big mouth shut?"

"Well, let's not play," Howard suggested. "Let's just call it off."

"That's right," said Charles. "Then we can dig some more. Maybe we'll find something else." He apparently thought that the whole baseball field was full of treasures.

The other four turned angrily on the twins.

"Nothing doing," Buster said. "We're in this, and you guys have to stick with us."

"All right, all right," said Howard. "It was just

a suggestion. But what are we going to do?"

"Well, we'll have to do *something,*" said Johnny. "Why can't we get some more guys? We ought to, anyhow."

Buster shook his head. "We've already asked everybody else in our class that would be any use. Either they have to take music lessons or help their father in the store, or else their mothers won't let them go out to your place."

"Well, what about somebody in some other class?" Johnny asked.

"Who?"

Johnny thought a minute. He looked around the yard. Suddenly he pointed. Two boys were walking out together. One was small and thin. The other was several inches taller and quite plump. The small one was tossing a ball up in the air and catching it as he walked. The fat one had a fielder's mitt strapped to his belt. They looked to Johnny like the answer to a prayer.

"Why don't we ask them?" he inquired.

The other boys shook their heads. "They're only in the fifth grade," said Buster. "Anyhow, they wouldn't want to."

"How do you know?" Johnny asked.

"Well, they never go with us. They always go together," said Buster.

"We never asked them," Johnny said. "Come on, let's ask them now."

"But how do you know they can play?" Joe asked.

"Oh, rats," said Johnny. "They can learn. At least they can field." He didn't stop to argue any longer but ran after the two boys.

"Hey, you guys!" he called.

The two boys stopped.

"You want to play ball with us?" Johnny asked.

The two boys looked suspiciously at each other and then at Johnny and the group standing on the steps.

"Us? Play with you?" the small one asked.

"Sure. What's your name?"

"Pat," said the boy. "And he's Lorenzo."

"Well, what do you say?"

"You mean it?" Lorenzo asked.

"Well, I asked you, didn't I?" said Johnny.

"I thought maybe you were kidding," said Lorenzo.

"No, we're not," said Johnny. "If you want to play with us, go home fast and find out if you can come out to my place."

Again the boys looked at each other. Then Lorenzo nodded at Pat. Pat grinned and said, "OK, we'll ask our mothers."

"Meet us over at the college," said Johnny. "We'll wait for you."

The two boys rushed off like bullets shot out of a gun. The Willow Creek Braves proceeded to meet Jackson.

"I told you they'd come," Johnny said. Inwardly he was a little doubtful. Maybe they would be no good at all, and it was too near time for the game to start teaching them everything. But no, he told himself. There must be *something* they could do.

Jackson was waiting at the curb. He was a little surprised when he learned that two more boys were coming. He wasn't sure they would fit into the jeep. But there was nothing to be done except pack them in. Pat and Lorenzo came running up the street. Pat was far in advance. Lorenzo was puffing heavily behind. They both had grins on their faces.

"We can go," Pat announced as soon as he was within half a block of them.

They all jammed themselves into the jeep.

"Wait," said Jackson. He got a rope and tied it around the body of the jeep. "There. That will

Jackson wasn't sure they would fit into the jeep

hold you in. Now everybody hang on and we'll start."

Ten minutes later they were running across the field.

"Get in position for batting practice," said Jackson. "Joe, Max and Howard in the field. You two new boys get in line. Let's see what you can do. Johnny, you lead off."

Johnny picked up the bat.

"Four chances, everybody," said Jackson. "Bunt the first, then swat the rest."

Johnny laid down a meek little bunt right at Jackson's feet. Then when the next one came he laid into it and sent it flying toward the woods. Joe jumped for it and it sailed over his head. He started to run after it. When he had found it, Jackson called him over.

"I couldn't reach it," Joe said. "He hit it too high."

"Wait a minute," said Jackson. "What do you think this practice is for?"

"So we'll know what to do in a real game," said Joe.

"And do they have high ones in a real game?" Jackson asked.

"Sure."

"Well, then, when you see a high one, too high to jump for, you turn around and run with it. Get that?"

"Yes." Without another word Joe trotted back to his place.

Johnny finished his turn at bat. Now it was Pat's turn. Everybody watched to see what he would do. Pat was small and thin. He looked almost too small to handle Johnny's big bat. When the pitch came, he hit it a short, hard whack, right between Max and Howard, and began to run.

He ran like a streak. He got all around the bases while Max and Howard were still trying to decide whose ball it was.

"Zowie!" Johnny yelled. "He can run all right."

Lorenzo was next. He took his place at bat and said, apologetically, "I can't run so fast."

"Well, let's see if you can hit," said Jackson.

"I can hit a little," said Lorenzo. He stood awkwardly. He seemed top-heavy. He let a couple of Jackson's pitches go by, and then he clouted the ball. It went up into the air and seemed to be going into the woods. But Pat had turned and run the minute the ball was hit. He was going as fast as the ball.

The only difference was that he was on the ground. But when he was nearly at the woods he leaped into the air and came down holding the ball.

The other boys let go with a cheer. They swarmed around the two new boys and pounded them on their backs.

"Jumping grasshoppers!" Johnny yelled. "We've got a couple of ballplayers! We're saved."

"Oh, we're not really so good," Pat said. "I can't throw so well and I can't bat. I guess I haven't got enough muscle."

"But you can run like a streak, and Lorenzo can hit like—like Ted Williams," said Johnny. "Where'd you learn that?"

"Oh, we just play with each other," Pat explained. "We never got to play in any games."

"Well, why didn't you ask us?"

"We didn't think you'd want us," said Pat.

"Didn't think we'd want you!" yelled Johnny "Jumping grasshoppers! They're crazy!"

But suddenly he remembered something. He remembered the day he had tried to get his friends to go over and ask to play with the Oak Street bunch. And the way he himself had been given the cold shoulder.

Maybe if these boys had come up and offered their services, he and his gang *would* have turned them down.

He hoped not. They would have been foolish if they had.

He grinned. "Well, maybe you aren't crazy," he said. "Anyhow, we sure do need you. Don't we, guys?"

The other Braves grinned, too. "You bet," they said.

"And now that you've got that settled," said Jackson, "let's go on playing ball."

13. Ready for the Game

THEY went back to their batting practice. Jackson pitched all kinds of balls; high ones, low ones, fast ones, slow ones. He told each Brave exactly what was the matter with his hitting and made him go back and do it over until he was satisfied.

After that they practiced their throwing and catching, and then they practiced base-running.

At last, Jackson called time out for a rest.

The Braves dropped thankfully to the ground and wiped the sweat off their faces.

"Golly, Jackson," Joe complained, "you sure do make us work hard."

"I was under the impression you had a few things to learn," said Jackson. "There was a little matter

of a game you are supposed to play. By the way, where and when is this game going to take place?"

Nobody seemed to know.

"You boys need a captain," said Jackson.

"But we have you to tell us what to do," said Buster.

"Oh, no," Jackson said. "I only tell you how to play."

"Then," said Max, "let us have Johnny for captain. He is always telling us what to do, anyhow."

Johnny wasn't sure he liked that description of himself, but he did like being captain.

He appointed Joe to confer with his brother about the date for the game and to ask if they could use eight players, with Jackson to pitch for them but not to bat. He was also to suggest that the game be played out here on the Braves' field.

Suddenly Johnny happened to glance up at Lorenzo and Pat. They were looking at each other out of the sides of their eyes and they seemed unhappy.

"What's the matter?" he asked.

"Well–uh," said Pat, "we're not so awfully good. We never played with a team, and maybe we better not play–"

"Hey!" said Johnny. "You said you'd play. You can't back out now."

"But we don't want to be the cause of you losing the game."

"Now, listen here," said Jackson. "Gather round, boys. I'm going to make a speech. And every one of you get it through your head."

He seemed very serious.

"What's coming?" Johnny wondered. "Is he getting tired of coaching us? Did we do something to make him mad?"

Jackson was speaking again. "Now you like to play ball, don't you?"

They all nodded solemnly.

"But you haven't had as much chance to play as the boys over on Oak Street, have you?"

They shook their heads.

"So you naturally can't be as good as they are."

More head shaking.

"So there's only one thing for you to do. And that is, be as good as you can. You're going to play them. Maybe you won't win. But you'll play the best game you know how and that's all. Get that?"

More nodding.

Jackson went on. "And there aren't going to be any hard feelings afterward. Nobody is going to say to anybody else, 'Aw, gee, if you'd only caught that fly ball, they wouldn't have made that extra run.' You're going to do the best you can and have a good time. Understand?"

"OK," said Johnny.

"Well, then," said Jackson, getting up off the ground and stretching, "as long as you understand, I'm going to teach you a few trick plays. Everybody up."

"Oh, boy!" said Joe. "Just like in the regular teams! Wait till I tell my—"

"Just a minute!" Jackson said. "You will please not tell your brother. If you do, you'll spoil everything."

"What do you mean, Coach?" Joe asked.

"Well," Jackson said, "it's not usual for kids your

age to use special plays or signals. I don't think the Oak Street boys use them. But since they have the advantage in age and playing, I don't think it would be unfair if you have a little advantage of your own. Now pay attention. And Joe, you'll soon see why you mustn't tell your brother."

It sounded exciting. Special plays! And signals!

"Now, Johnny," said Jackson, "you get up at bat. Pat, you're a fast runner so we'll say you are at first base. Now, Pat, I'm going to teach you how to steal."

"What!" Pat looked horrified.

"Don't worry." Jackson laughed. "It's perfectly legal, provided the other team does it, too. Johnny, you tell your scout to find out if they do. Now, Joe, you pitch. Naturally, I won't be pitching to you boys in the game. When you're at bat I'll be sitting on the side lines. Pat, you watch Joe get ready to pitch. Now, once the pitcher starts pitching, he has to go on with it. If he stops and tries to put a base runner out, instead, it's called—who knows?"

"A balk," said Johnny.

"Right. So as soon as he starts to pitch, you run like anything for second base."

Johnny swung and missed. Max caught the ball and threw it to second base

Joe wound up, and Pat ran like a rabbit. He was at second in a flash.

"Good," said Jackson. "Now go back to first."

Pat went back.

"Now the next time, don't steal unless you see me take my handkerchief out of my pocket and wipe my forehead. That will be the signal."

Joe got ready to pitch. Pat, with his eye first on Joe and then on Jackson, was on his toes, ready to leave the base. Jackson took out his handkerchief and wiped his brow. Pat ran. Johnny swung and missed.

Max caught the ball and threw to second base, but Pat was there ahead of it.

"Very good!" said Jackson.

"But does the batter have to swing?" Pat asked. "The ball might be no good."

"No, he doesn't," said Jackson. "Not on a steal. But on another play he does. It's called—"

"Hit and run," said Johnny.

"My, that boy knows everything," said Jackson. "All right, suppose you tell us about it."

"It's just what you said," said Johnny. "The batter has to swing. The runner runs with the pitch. What's your signal going to be?"

"Well, suppose I scratch my left elbow," said Jackson. "We'll let Buster be the base runner this time. And, Howard, you be the batter."

Buster went to first base. Jackson, on the sidelines, acted as if his left elbow had suddenly begun to itch. He scratched it violently. Joe pitched, Howard swung and Buster ran to second base.

"But why does the batter have to swing?" Buster asked. "He might get a ball that he can't hit, and that would mean a strike on him."

"He has to take a chance," said Jackson. "He swings because it obscures the catcher's view so the catcher can't get hold of the ball and put the runner out. It's to protect the runner. We'll use it if we very much need a run."

"Do we always have to wait for the signal?" Johnny asked.

"Better," said Jackson. "Of course, you could steal on your own, but you don't know how these boys play. I'll be in a better position to watch than you."

"But will this be fair?" Max asked. "The poor Oak Street boys do not have a coach. Maybe they will lose the game."

"That's one of the things we want," said Johnny.

"We're not playing them just to make them feel good, you zany."

"Zany!" said Max. "What is this? A new kind of bird?"

"Yeah. Looks just like you," said Johnny. "Come on. Let's do the hit and run again."

Max looked scared. "You hit me and I run, ha?"

Johnny chased him around the field a couple of times until Jackson called them back.

"One more thing. A double steal," he said. "This time we'll have men on first and third. Pat, you go to third. Howard, on first. Charles, at bat. Now, when you see me pick up a small stone and throw it up and catch it, you both run with the pitch. Batter doesn't have to swing."

Joe pitched. The two runners started off. Max caught the ball and flung it to second base. Howard fled back to first base, but the ball was there ahead of him and he was out. But Pat got safely home.

"Suppose the catcher holds the ball or throws it to third to put out the runner there?" Charles asked.

"Then the guy from first base gets safely to second," said Johnny. "Don't you see? Either way we gain a base."

"Right," said Jackson. "Now, one more thing.

When our team is at bat, I want those who aren't batting to be at the bases, coaching."

"But you're the coach, Jackson," said Max. "Is everybody going to be coaches now?"

"I'm the head coach," said Jackson. "But when a runner gets to a base, he often doesn't know whether to run for the next base or stay where he is. He doesn't know where the ball is because he's been busy running. So if one of his teammates is there to tell him, it's a big help. See?"

"Ach, sure," said Max. "We get so smart, maybe we even win the game."

"If you win," Jackson said, "you get a big reward."

"Oh, boy!" The boys crowded around him. "What is it? Huh, Jackson? What's the reward?"

But Jackson shut his lips. He wouldn't tell. "You'll find out," was all he would say.

"But if we lose?" Johnny asked.

"Then you'll find out, too," said Jackson. "OK, men, dismissed."

14. Willow Creek Braves vs. Oak Street

AND NOW, at last, it was Saturday. *The* Saturday. The day Johnny had been waiting for. He had thought he wouldn't be able to wait until this day came. And now that it was here, he just couldn't sit still. He was tense.

He had been up since six o'clock. He couldn't stay in bed. Jackson had told the boys to get a good long sleep. But after tossing around in his bed for an hour, Johnny had decided that he was just wearing himself out trying to get rested, so he got up

and went out to feed the chickens.

"This is the day we play our game," he told the chickens. "This is me. I'm up at bat, see, and there are two men on base and two out and I swing at the ball—"

He grabbed an imaginary bat and swung at an invisible ball. The chickens fled squawking to the other end of the yard.

Johnny picked up the pail of eggs and started back to the house. On the way he met Ted Williams, coming back from his night's hunting.

"Hi, Ted," he greeted him. "Catch anything?"

Ted did not answer. He rubbed himself against Johnny's leg and yawned.

"Oh, you won't talk, eh?" said Johnny. "Well, all right. I just wanted to tell you, this is the day of our game. You better be out there on the field if you want to see something good."

Ted walked off. Johnny went into the kitchen. His mother was up at last, mixing pancake batter.

"Morning, Mom," said Johnny. "You going to see our game?"

"Of course, I am, dear," she answered. "But why are you up so early? There's nothing to get so excited about."

Funny, nobody seemed to understand how he felt. Well, the Braves would. For a week and a half they had been practicing every single day. They had worked hard. There had been no fooling. They were acting like a team now. They knew each other's weaknesses and strong points. They had worked out their line-up together. Nobody had complained about Pat being up first, or Lorenzo fourth, right after Johnny, though they were newcomers. Even Joe hadn't said a word about being sixth. And not once had Howard or Charles suggested playing Indians instead. They meant business.

But still, Johnny felt jittery. After all, he was responsible. It had all been his idea in the first place. He had kept the team going when they would have stopped. He was always telling them what to do, as Max said. He wanted them to make a good showing so that they would want to keep on and not get discouraged.

Slowly the morning passed. Johnny helped his father in the store. He took care of the gas pumps. Lunch time came and went.

A car drove up and its horn tooted. Johnny went to see what was wanted. But the people were getting out. It was Max and his aunt and uncle. Max's round face was shining and red with excitement.

"I haf bring my aunt and oncle," he said, with more accent than usual. Then he dragged them off to see the club house.

A minute later another car stopped. It was Buster with his parents and kid brother. Then the twins arrived with their parents. Jumping grasshoppers! They were going to have a big crowd!

More cars arrived. They lined up on both sides

of the road. Johnny's mother came out. The mothers got together and talked. The fathers were busy carrying out boxes and chairs for the ladies to sit on.

The Willow Creek Braves got together in the stone house. They jigged around, punched each other and pretended to hit home runs.

But where were the Oak Street boys? What if they didn't show up?

"What if Jackson forgot to go for them?" said Howard.

"Don't be a dope," Buster said. "He wouldn't forget. But maybe some of them fell out of the jeep."

"Maybe he had a flat tire or ran out of gas," Joe said.

Johnny tried to calm them down, though he didn't feel calm.

"They'll get here. Don't you worry. Old Jackson will get 'em here. He never failed us yet and he won't now."

At last another horn tooted and a flash of red went past the windows, and after it a truck.

Joe gave a yell. "That's my father's truck!" he shouted. "He brought them! Yay!"

The boys piled out of the truck as the Braves ran

to greet them. Johnny, as Captain and host, went first.

The big boys didn't have much to say. They looked around, a bit suspiciously at first, as if they were not quite sure what they had let themselves in for. Jackson escorted Joe's father out to the field, with Daniel Boone running ahead of him, while the Braves led their guests into the club house. The Oak Street boys noted the pennants on the walls, the gloves hanging on either side of the fireplace and the bats stacked in a corner.

Tony turned to his brother. "This is all right," he admitted.

"I told you it was," Joe said. "And I can tell you a few other things, too. Our coach—"

The Braves heard him. They looked at Johnny. Johnny nodded to Max, who was closest to Joe. Max bumped into Joe.

"Oh, excuse me," he said. "I am so clumsy today!"

Joe gave him an annoyed look but he didn't say any more. He just bent over to fix his sock, as if it needed attention.

Jackson put his head in at the door. "If you boys are ready," he said, "we'll get going."

The boys hitched up their trousers, stuffed their shirts in, tightened their shoelaces and pounded their gloves. Then they walked out into the sunshine and ran onto the field. A cheer rose from the parents on the sidelines.

Daniel Boone ran out in front, his head up, his tail waving, as if he knew he was the mascot.

"Good old Daniel," said Johnny, patting him. "You brought us luck once. Now see that you do it again."

"Never mind luck," said Jackson. "It's sweat that counts now."

"OK, coach," said Johnny.

He turned to Tony Palo. "You're up first. Want to use our bats or your own?"

"We'll try them all out," said Tony.

"OK," said Johnny. "Want to take a few minutes to warm up?"

Tony nodded. Johnny threw him a ball, and the Braves sat down while the visitors tossed it back and forth, batted a few and then stepped aside to let the home team have their turn.

When they had finished, Johnny turned to the onlookers. "We need an umpire," he said.

"I'll volunteer," his father said. Johnny had been

hoping he would. But then he thought of something else.

"Maybe be should have two umpires," he said to Tony. "Do you think your father would be one?"

Mr. Palo jumped up. "Certainly," he said. "I've got one boy on each team, so I'll make a good umpire. I'll have to be fair."

"Swell," said Johnny, "and remember, fellows, what the umpire says, counts."

"But what if the umpires can't agree?" Buster asked.

"Then we'll let them fight it out," said Johnny.

"That I would like to see," Jackson said. He pulled out of his pocket a brand new ball, snow-white and shiny, and threw it to Mr. Palo. Mr. Palo examined it and tossed it back to Jackson, who walked to his position on the pitching mound. The Braves took their places; Max, ready to catch, behind the plate, Johnny at first base, Buster at second and Joe at third. Pat was shortstop. Howard was in left field, Charles in center and Lorenzo in right field.

Michael Brown stepped up to the plate and swung his bat a few times.

"Play ball!" Mr. Palo called, and the game was on.

Jackson pitched a hard, fast ball. Michael swung at it.

"Strike!" the umpire called.

Another fast ball.

"Strike two!"

Then the third pitch.

This time Michael swung and hit hard. The ball struck the ground halfway between Lorenzo and Buster. They both ran for it and Michael got to first base before they could decide which of them was to throw it to Johnny. Michael turned and grinned at Johnny.

Johnny scowled. This was a fine beginning.

"You guys look alive there," he called to Buster and Lorenzo.

The next man up for Oak Street was Bill Anderson, a tall, skinny boy. When the pitch came to him, he slashed at it at once and got safely to first base, while Michael galloped on to second.

This was terrible.

A boy named George Swenson was up third.

"Come on, guys," Johnny pleaded. "Don't let this guy get on base, too."

But George got a single, and Michael scored.

There were men on first and second now, and Tony came up to bat.

Tony wasn't in a hurry to hit. He waited for a couple of pitches to go by, and then he swung. It was a good hard hit and the two men already on base raced on. The ball sailed on to left field. It looked like another base hit for sure, and Johnny groaned, dancing on his base and wishing he could get loose to snag that ball. Charles was just standing still in left field, looking at the ball, and Buster was afraid to leave his base.

Suddenly little Pat was running. He was going as fast as the ball, only he was on the ground. Now the ball was coming down and Pat was under it. He had it. He whirled around and threw to Buster, and Buster caught it an instant before Bill got back to second base. Bill and Tony were out.

The Braves grinned at each other across the field.

The Oak Street boys were a little annoyed. It was clear that they had expected to walk off with the game, and here they had two men out already. Then the next boy hit a weak one to right field and was out at first base. That retired the side.

Now Willow Creek was up. Pat walked to the plate and stood there, holding the big bat, while

Tony, the Oak Street pitcher, looked him over. It was clear that Tony thought of Pat as a harmless little boy who couldn't hit anything. His first pitch was fast but right where Pat could reach it. Pat gave the ball a poke right between the pitcher and the third baseman. Then he was off. He was at first base before anybody knew what had happened.

Max was next. He looked anxiously at Johnny. "What should I do?" he asked.

"Do anything you can," said Johnny. "If you get a chance to bunt, do it. Even if you're out, Pat will get ahead."

Max nodded. "I try. I like my aunt and oncle to see me get on the base, but it is better for the team if Pat gets ahead."

He walked to the plate. He was the picture of the nervous batter who doesn't know what he is doing. He dropped the bat on his toe. He hopped around, holding his foot in his hand. He waved to his aunt.

He looked around at the catcher and said, "You watch out that I do not hit you with the bat."

"Yeah?" said the catcher. "Well, if you do hit me, it'll be the only thing you *will* hit."

"You are a person, not a thing," said Max. "But

He was the picture of the nervous batter

still I do not wish to hit you. It is against the rules."

Then he bent over and waited for the pitch. When it came, he swung his bat as if it were a hatchet, and simply knocked the ball down on the ground. Then he jumped over it and galloped for first base. The catcher was so surprised that he couldn't get hold of it for a moment, and that moment was what Max needed. He beat the throw to first base, while Pat raced for second.

Now Johnny was up. If I can only knock those two in! he thought. Boy, oh boy! Two runs in the first inning. I won't care if we don't get anything else.

He squinted at the pitcher. Here was the ball. He swung. He heard a crack. He didn't know where the ball was, where anything was, but he flung the bat from him and ran. The first baseman was waving his arms at somebody, but Howard, who was coaching at first, shouted to Johnny, "Go on, don't stop!"

Johnny went on. When he got to second base, he saw Joe signaling to him to come on to third. He kept going.

"OK," said Joe when he got there. "They've got the ball now."

Johnny stopped and looked around. Pat and Max had just scored. Lorenzo was stepping up to the plate. Johnny forgot what he had thought a few minutes ago.

"If he would only knock me in," he said to himself, "I wouldn't care if I never made any more runs."

Lorenzo took his awkward stance, gave his bat a shake and swung. It was a two-bagger! Johnny ran home.

The Willow Creek Braves cheered.

Suddenly from the road there came the screech of brakes and the tooting of a horn. Then a man came running across the field toward them. It was Professor Sedgwick.

"Wait!" he called. "Why didn't you tell me what time the game was starting? I've got to see it, too!"

"Why, Father!" Jackson exclaimed. "You said baseball was the great American time-waster!"

"Rubbish!" snapped the Professor. "I told you I'd changed my mind. Now let's see you play."

15.

The End of the Game

THE PROFESSOR took a seat beside Mrs. Burton, who tried to explain to him what was happening.

Buster was up now. The Oak Street boys were determined not to let any more runs get through. Tony gave Buster a couple of fast balls. After that there were a couple of fouls, and then Buster hit one that popped straight up in the air and Tony caught it.

Then Joe and Howard struck out.

As the Oak Street team walked off the field, Mr. Palo announced the score. "At the end of the first inning, the Willow Creek Braves, three; Oak Street, one."

Jackson went back to the pitching mound, and the first batter walked to the plate.

"Come on, Jackson," Johnny called. "Let's get this one out."

But now the Oak Street boys were on their toes. They hit everything they could. The Braves did their best but they couldn't prevent their opponents from getting two runs in the second inning and two more in the third. Now it was five to three.

It stayed that way all through the fourth and fifth innings. By the end of the first half of the sixth, the Oak Street boys had three more runs. It was eight to three. The Braves were feeling downcast. It certainly didn't look too good.

Joe seemed to feel worse than the rest because he hadn't been able to do anything against his brother's team. Now Joe was at bat. He looked glumly at Tony on the mound.

Tony grinned at him.

"Come on, shrimp," he taunted him. "Hit this."

Johnny, watching them, saw Joe's face get red. He looked angry. He swung back and hit with all his might. He threw down the bat and ran. He was at second base when Johnny motioned to him to stop.

It looked as if Joe had a chance to score. But Howard and Charles were next up. Neither of them could hit very well.

Howard walked timidly to the plate. He didn't like to bat. He was always afraid the ball would hit him. Instead of leaning into it, he shrank back.

Joe took a couple of steps off second base. He was watching Jackson and Howard. Jackson was taking a handkerchief out of his pocket and rubbing his eye with it. That wasn't quite the signal, but it was close enough.

Tony wound up and pitched, and Joe was off like a bullet out of a gun. The catcher shot the ball over to the third baseman, but too late. Joe was safe.

Tony turned around and stared at his brother.

"Whaddya know!" he exclaimed. "The kid stole a base!"

Joe grinned. Then he yelled at Howard. "Come on, Howard, let's see you hit!"

Howard grinned back. He set his jaw. When the next pitch came, he didn't shrink back. He looked at it and decided he didn't like it, and let it go by. Then he smacked the next one as hard as he could.

It was a ground ball. The right fielder thought he had it, but it bounced away from him and he had to run for it. Howard rounded first and went on to second, and Joe scored.

His teammates grabbed him. "That was nice work, Joey!" Johnny said. "What made you decide to steal?"

"Decide!" said Joe. "Jackson gave me the signal!"

"Why, no, I didn't," said Jackson.

"I saw you take your handkerchief out of your pocket," Joe insisted.

"Did I rub my forehead with it?" Jackson asked.

"No," said Joe, "but I didn't think that was so important."

Jackson began to laugh. "I had something in my eye!" he roared. "Well, it was a good job. Joe, you're OK. It's eight to four now. If we can make a couple more runs before the end of the game, it will be a good job."

"Play ball!" the two umpires shouted. "How long is this conference going on?"

The boys began to yell at Charles. "Come on, knock your brother in!"

But Charles got excited and struck out. Pat was put out at first and Max grounded out. In spite of those three quick outs, however, the Braves felt better now. That run of Joe's had proved they could still do something.

When Johnny came up in the seventh inning, he hit the first pitch for a double.

Now Lorenzo walked to the plate.

"Come on, Lorenzo," Johnny called. "You hit me home before. Do it again." Tony glanced at Johnny over his shoulder. Then he gave his attention to Lorenzo. He put lots of speed into the pitch. But Lorenzo put all his weight into his swing, and when the ball met his bat, it simply started going the other way twice as fast. For Johnny, it would have been a home run, but for Lorenzo it was a triple. Johnny scored easily. Eight to five now and nobody out. Buster was next.

Then Johnny had an idea. "Time out!" he called.

He whispered to Buster: "Look, Buster, you bunt this time if you can."

Buster shook his head. "I can't bunt," he said. "That's Max's specialty."

"But do it," said Johnny. "Bunt over toward the first base line if you get the right kind of ball. That'll help Lorenzo get home. He's such a slow runner."

"But that will probably put me out," Buster objected.

"Yes," said Johnny, "but we need the run."

"OK," said Buster.

He missed a couple. Then Tony sent him a slow ball and he managed to bunt. Buster was put out, but Lorenzo came puffing across the plate, beaming with joy. He had made a run!

Johnny felt wonderful. He felt that he was really being captain of the team. He looked across at his mother. She was explaining to Professor Sedgwick what had happened.

"It's called a sacrifice bunt," she said. "Buster sacrificed so that the other boy could score."

"Why, that's very good!" the Professor said. "That's fine training for boys. Learning to give up something for the sake of the team! Why, this is a useful game!"

"Of course it is," said Mrs. Burton. "And our boys are doing very well. The score is eight to six. They're only two runs behind."

"Behind!" cried the Professor. "Why aren't they ahead? They ought to win. Jackson! Come here at once. Why aren't our boys winning?"

"*Sh,* Father," said Jackson. "They're doing the

best they can. Don't make them nervous."

"Who's making them nervous?" the Professor shouted. "I just want them to go out there and win!"

Johnny gathered his team together. "Listen, men," he said, "the Professor thinks we're wonderful. Come on. Let's show him what we can do. Joe, you're up next. Don't let your brother get you rattled. We've only got one out."

Joe did his best. But Tony was determined not to let his kid brother get any more hits. Joe finally did connect with a ball, but it was foul and the first baseman caught it easily. Then Howard got scared and struck out. That made three.

"Never mind," said Johnny. "We've still got two innings left. Now go on out there and don't let them get anything if you can help it."

The boys walked slowly out to their positions. They were a little tired. It was a harder game than they had ever played.

But not harder, Johnny thought, than fighting Indians a hundred and fifty years ago. Johnny walked to first base and slapped his glove against the old willow stump.

"You just watch this game," he told the stump.

"Jackson! Why aren't our boys winning?"

"And a hundred and fifty years from now you can remember it."

Then he turned his attention to Jackson.

Jackson pitched carefully. The first Oak Street batter was a short, stocky boy, named Phil. After a couple of balls and a strike, he swatted the ball right down the first base line. It was going fast, but Johnny got right in front of it. He held out his glove, and clapped his bare hand over it and put his foot on the base. The speed of the ball nearly knocked him over, but he got his balance and waited for the advancing runner. The runner was in such a hurry, though, that he bumped into Johnny and the two of them rolled on the ground.

"Safe!" the Oak Street team yelled.

"He is not!" shouted the Braves. "Johnny put the ball on him."

Both umpires raced over. Johnny had the ball tight in his hand. Phil was out.

Johnny jumped to his feet, wiping sweat and dirt in streaks down his face. The next batter got on base. The third, also. Then Michael was up again.

Michael wasn't going to be struck out. He hit a high one toward first. The men on first and second started to run. Johnny hesitated a second. He saw Lorenzo in right field starting for the ball. Lorenzo couldn't get there in time. Johnny turned and ran. The ball began to drop. Johnny took a quick look backward, put up his glove and caught it.

"Take it, Buster!" he yelled, shooting the ball to him. Buster, with his foot on second base, caught the ball and put the runner out.

"Double play!" Mr. Palo called. "That makes three out!"

The Braves joyfully threw down their gloves, and the Oak Street team glumly walked out to the field.

Charles went to the plate. He picked up the bat. He had looked relieved at the end of the seventh, when Howard had struck out in time so that he hadn't had to bat. But now he was in a worse position. He had to lead off. He looked around at Johnny for comfort.

"Go on, Charles," said Johnny. "Get us a hit. You can do it."

The Oak Street catcher heard. He laughed. "Hey, Tony!" he called to his pitcher. "Look out for this batter. They say he can hit!"

Tony laughed, too. Johnny saw Charles look scared.

I bet he wishes he were playing Indians, Johnny thought.

"Come on, Charles," he yelled. "Get on the warpath! Yahoo!"

Charles seemed to feel better. He grabbed his bat like a tomahawk. When the ball came, he sliced at it. It popped up in the air, dropped, took a crazy hop and landed between the pitcher and the third baseman. Charles got safely to first.

Pat also hit a single, while Charles got to second. But then Max hit a fly which Tony caught and shot to second base to put Pat out.

The Oak Street boys called out to each other across the field. "Two out! Come on, guys, get this next one and we'll be up."

Johnny picked up the bat. Eight to six, and two out! He saw his mother and the Professor talking again. The Professor looked gloomy. His mother was smiling cheerfully. He knew that smile. It was the kind that meant that he shouldn't get too discouraged. Even if they lost, she would understand. Well, maybe they *would* lose. But not if *he* could help it. He clenched his fingers around the bat. Here came the pitch.

Johnny swung—and missed.

"Strike!" Mr. Palo called.

"Ha!" laughed Michael. "Come on, Tony, two more."

"That's what you think," Johnny muttered. He waited for the next pitch. He swung. There was a sharp crack. The ball sailed across the field. Johnny ran for first base.

"Run, Johnny!" his teammates yelled. "Keep going!"

Johnny went on. He rounded second base. Ahead of him he could see Charles crossing the plate. He rounded third.

"A home run! Yay!"

Johnny fell on the ground and panted. The rest

of the Braves did a war dance around him. Two or three of them fell on top of him. He didn't care. The score was tied now.

Even after Lorenzo was put out right after that on account of his slow running, the Braves still felt fine.

All through the first half of the ninth the score remained tied. The fans were more excited now, especially the mothers. They had come, resigned to sitting through nine innings in the hot sun, just to please their sons. Now they were getting up to see better. They had stopped talking to each other about recipes for soup or how to make their children go to bed on time. They were paying attention.

The Braves clustered around Jackson.

"You have a chance to win this game, kids," he said. "Don't get excited. Even if you don't win it this inning, it will still be tied, and maybe we'll get some runs in the tenth. So be careful. Don't get wild."

He went and sat down, and Buster, first up, walked to the plate.

Buster was going to be careful. He eyed Tony warily. Then came the pitch. Buster swung. It was a clean hit to center field. Buster stopped on first and Joe came up. Buster watched carefully. Joe wiped his hands on his pants and picked up the bat.

Over on the sidelines, Jackson was standing up. He lifted his left elbow and looked at it and scratched it. It looked as if he had just had a bad bite—to anybody but a Willow Creek Brave.

To Buster it meant something else. Joe had seen the signal, too, and Joe was going to hit. Tony was pitching now. The instant Tony's arm started to move, Buster was off. Joe hit to right field and raced for first. Buster crossed second. The right fielder was scrambling for the ball. Buster was halfway to third. The fielder was throwing. Buster threw himself down and slid into base a split second ahead of the ball. Joe was on first.

The crowd cheered. The Oak Street team looked puzzled. These kids were certainly better than they had expected.

Howard and Charles, though, were easy to strike out. Now Pat came up.

Johnny, coaching near third base, wished hard. "I hope you don't strike out, too," he muttered. "Come on, Pat! Two men on base! Let's break up the game!"

The two base runners were watching Jackson,

standing back of home plate. Jackson had a little stone in his hand. He kept throwing it up in the air and catching it. He looked nervous—to anybody but a Willow Creek Brave. To Buster on third and to Joe on first it meant something else. It was going to be a double steal.

Tony wound up. There went the ball and there went Joe. Michael, the catcher, looked quickly from Buster, who was taking a lead off third, to Joe, streaking for second. If he got Joe out at second, that would be the third out and the game would still be tied. He shot the ball to the second baseman. But Joe wasn't going to be tagged. He turned back to first. Buster started for home and slid across the plate in a cloud of dust and with a big hole in the seat of his pants.

The game was over: Willow Creek, nine; Oak Street, eight!

16.

Rewards!

A CROWD of yelling, dirty, happy boys swarmed around Jackson. They jumped on him and on each other, shouting with joy.

"We won! Yay! We won! Hooray!"

Their mothers and fathers crowded around them. Buster's little brother grabbed Buster's fielding glove and tried it on.

Howard's baby sister was scared by the commotion and began to cry.

Daniel Boone barked wildly, running back and forth with his tongue hanging out and his tail wagging.

Johnny squeezed through the crowd to his mother.

She was standing beside the Professor, who was shaking her hand up and down exclaiming, "That's a fine game! I must learn that game! Excellent for character-building!" As soon as he caught sight of Johnny he began to shake *his* hand.

"I will get Andrew to teach me that game," he said.

Johnny was glad the Professor was so interested but he wanted a drink more than anything else.

"Hey, Mom!" he said. "We're thirsty. Can't we have some drinks?"

"Of course!" his mother said. "We're going to celebrate. Soda pop and lemonade for everybody."

Sure enough, Mr. Burton and Mr. Palo were coming from the house, each bending under the weight of two big buckets of cracked ice, filled with bottles of soda.

"This way, everybody!" Mr. Burton called.

He set down his buckets under the big willow, behind the stone house. He began to open bottles and hand them around. Soon they were all tipping bottles up to their mouths and eating cookies—all but the Oak Street boys.

Suddenly Johnny noticed that they were standing off by themselves, with their bats and gloves gath-

Suddenly Johnny noticed that the Oak Street boys were standing off by themselves

ered up, as if they were getting ready to go.

"Hey, what's the matter with you guys?" Johnny called, running up to them. "Come and have some drinks."

He grabbed Tony's arm and dragged him over to the willow.

"We didn't know you'd have enough," Tony muttered.

"You're crazy," Johnny told him gracefully. "Pop, will you open a few more bottles?"

The Oak Street boys put down their equipment and sat on the ground. The Braves sat down with them. There was silence, broken only by the gurgle of liquid being poured out of bottles into dry throats.

Then Tony said, "This is a pretty nice place you're got here."

"I told you—" his brother Joe began eagerly.

Max accidentally fell over on top of Joe.

"Oh, excuse me, Joe," he apologized. "I am so tired from my bunting. I did not see you there."

Joe gave Max a disgusted look and kept quiet.

"I'm glad you like it," said Johnny, ignoring the interruption. "At first, the fellows didn't want to come way out here. But now—"

"Oh, it isn't so far," said Michael. "What's a couple of miles?"

"It's far if you have to walk both ways," Buster said.

"Not if you have a bicycle," Tony said.

"And you kids sure do play better than we thought you would," Bill Anderson added. "Gee, I never thought you'd beat us."

"I guess that's what comes from having a coach," Tony said.

Johnny was puzzled. He didn't know what they were getting at. He was glad they liked the place and he was glad they thought well of the Braves and their coach. But all these compliments weren't being passed out for no reason.

"Any time you want to play us again," he said, "just let us know."

"You bet!" said Joe. "We'll play you any time."

"We'll go over to your lot the next time, if you want," Johnny offered.

The Oak Street boys just sat there and glanced at each other. Some kind of message was being telegraphed back and forth.

At last Tony said, "We'll play you. But we can't play in our lot."

"Why not?" Johnny asked, surprised.

The Oak Street boys looked unhappy. They looked angry. Johnny began to wonder what he had said to make them mad.

Then Tony explained. "It's been sold."

"Sold! What's been sold? What do you mean?"

"Our lot, where we play ball."

"But how could they sell it?"

"Why not? There's been a sign on it for years. But nobody ever paid any attention to it. We used it for a backstop. Now they've taken down the sign and put up one that says 'No Trespassing.' We've got no place to play."

They sat silent, waiting for Johnny to speak.

Johnny knew what was the matter. They were remembering the day when they had told him to go and play with somebody his own size. He grinned.

"Well, why don't you come out here and play?" he offered. "There's plenty of room."

"Gosh!" said Tony. "You mean it?"

"Sure," said Johnny. "Only, how would you get out here? Jackson can't take everybody in his jeep."

"We have bicycles," said Tony. "Golly, that would be swell. You sure your father won't mind?"

"Of course not," said Johnny. "It'll be much

better. We'll have enough guys for two teams and we can play games all the time. Only, of course, we don't play as well as you do."

"That's all right," Michael said hurriedly. "We can mix the teams, so we don't have too many kids—I mean, so we have some of you and some of us on each team."

"Now you're talking," said Johnny. "Come on. Let's ask Jackson what he thinks."

He jumped up and the rest of the boys got up, too, and followed him to where Jackson and the Professor stood in the center of a circle. Jackson was showing his father how to bat. Mr. Burton stood with the ball ready to pitch, and the Professor swung the bat over his shoulder and hit himself in the back with it.

"What's wrong with this club?" he demanded, rubbing himself.

"Nothing, Father," said Jackson. "You just haven't had much practice."

"Well, when do you come out to practice again?" the Professor asked. "I'll be here."

"Monday afternoon," said Jackson. He turned and saw the crowd of boys. "Well, boys, what do you say? Shall we allow Professor Sedgwick to join

the team?"

"Sure," said Johnny. "And we have a lot more guys here who want to join."

"Who?" Jackson asked.

"The Oak Street boys," said Johnny. "Would you mind? That is, would that be too many for you to coach?"

"Swell!" said Jackson. "The more the better! Glad to have you, fellows." He held out his hand to Tony, who shook it solemnly and then stepped back where he wouldn't be quite so noticeable. Johnny knew how he must feel with all those people looking at him.

He tried to think of something to change the subject. Suddenly an idea popped into his head.

"Hey, Jackson," he said. "Remember what you said last week?"

"No," said Jackson. "I said a lot of things. Which one are you thinking of?"

"You know," said Johnny. "You said we'd get a reward if we—that is—if—" Now *he* was embarrassed. He wished he hadn't brought that up. It wasn't so tactful to talk about getting a reward for winning the game. "Oh, skip it," he finished. "Let's all go and get some more drinks."

But Jackson apparently wasn't going to skip it. "Oh, yes," he said, smiling. "Now I remember. I said that if you kids won the game, you would have a reward."

Johnny was becoming more and more embarrassed. His face grew red.

"Yes, but never mind, Jackson. We don't care."

Jackson laughed. He went on. "But I didn't say what would happen to the *losing* team, did I?"

"No," said Johnny.

"Well, that's the surprise," said Jackson. "The

losing team gets a reward, too!"

"They do! You mean we both get it? What is it?" The boys all shouted at once.

Jackson held up his hand for silence. "Professor Sedgwick is giving the reward," he said. "It's his gift. Both teams are going to Cincinnati to see a Big League game."

At this the boys were speechless for a moment. And then the yell that burst forth was deafening. Both teams cheered for five minutes without stopping. Then, all grinning like jack-o'-lanterns, they surrounded the Professor and Jackson.

"When? When do we go? You mean we all go? How do we get there? What's it for?"

Jackson held up his hand again. "If you'll all sit down and keep quiet," he said, "I'll explain."

The boys sat down on the ground and listened.

"My father *used to hate* baseball," he said. "He used to think it was a waste of time. But after Johnny and his friends made their discovery about the stone house, he changed his mind. Now he approves of baseball. And, besides, he wants to say thank you. This is his way of doing it. Is that right, Father?"

"Yes," the Professor said. "And I want all you

boys to keep on playing. I'm going to watch you and see that you improve. And next Saturday, we're all going down to Cincinnati. We'll drive down. I'll drive my car and Mr. Burton will drive his—"

"You going, too, Pop?" Johnny broke in.

"I wouldn't miss it for anything," Mr. Burton said.

Johnny heaved a happy sigh. "It's going to be swell," he said.

The sun was far over in the west. The hens were cackling in their yard, announcing that it was suppertime. Far away across the fields a cow bell tinkled as a herd of cows walked slowly toward their barn. A breeze stirred the drooping branches of the willow tree. It was the peaceful time of the evening, when it would have been nice to sit and watch the sun go down.

But it was time to go home and get supper. The boys gathered up their bats and gloves again.

"You might as well leave your stuff in the club house," Johnny said to the Oak Street boys.

"OK," said Tony. "We'll see you Monday."

The grownups were gathering up empty bottles.

From out of the woods, finished with his day's

hunting and ready for his supper of canned salmon and milk, Ted Williams strolled. His tail waved gracefully in the air as he walked silently across the grass. Suddenly he stopped. He hadn't expected to see all those people. He changed his course. He headed over toward the farmhouse. But it was too late.

Daniel Boone, his ears flapping and his tongue hanging out, charged after him, sounding the battle cry.

"*Yi! Yi!*" he yelled.

Ted Williams stopped in his tracks and fuzzed his tail and spat. Daniel Boone didn't stop. He kept right on. He was going to get that cat this time.

Jackson shouted: "Daniel! Come here!" But Daniel paid no attention.

Ted changed his course again. He made straight for the willow tree. He dashed in among the people. His claws grabbed the bark of the tree. Like a gray streak of lightning he was up the tree and on the roof, and then, twisting his body, he disappeared into the hole over the door.

Daniel Boone looked all around. He couldn't see that cat anywhere. He barked and ran back and forth and then, determined to get it, he made a leap and fell into the water.

Jackson leaned over and pulled him out. Daniel shook himself, spraying water all around.

The ladies jumped out of the way.

"Drat that dog!" said Jackson. "I don't know what I keep him for. I'm going to tie him up!"

And he took him by the collar and prepared to drag him off.

"This time I mean it," he said.

Daniel twisted his head around and whined.

Johnny ran after them. "No, Jackson," he cried. "Don't tie him up. He hates it."

"But he's all wet," Jackson protested.

"That's all right, we'll dry him," said Johnny. He snatched up a sweatshirt and wrapped it around Daniel, tying the sleeves under the dog's chin. "We ought to be nice to him."

"What for, for goodness sake?" Jackson asked. "For chasing the cat, and not coming when I call him and falling in the water?"

"Sure," said Johnny. "Because look, Jackson—" he waved his arm at the field, the boys, the crowd of parents—"if it hadn't been for his chasing the cat and falling into the water, none of this would have happened."

Jackson grinned. "You're right," he said. "And the treasure would still be buried at first base."